CW00482016

John Stevens was born in London in 1969. He enjoyed writing when he was young and after a few professions and travelling extensively, he finally turned his hand to his childhood love of writing stories.

For my wonderful Jackie, without whom none of this could be possible and for helping me solve one of life's greatest mysteries.

For Tony (Bones) and Linda (Sunrise) for their love and support and for helping me through my darkest hour.

For my father, who would have loved this story and whose wisdom armed us all against the rigours of life.

Finally for my mother, Woo and Poz for being family and for never giving up on me.

John Stevens

THE CUCKOO HOWLS

AUSTIN MACAULEY PUBLISHERS™

LONDON • CAMBRIDGE • NEW YORK • SHARJAH

A CIP catalogue record for this title is available from the British Library.

ISBN 9781528902359 (Paperback)
ISBN 9781528902366 (Kindle e-book)
ISBN 9781528957236 (ePub e-book)

www.austinmacauley.com

First Published (2019)
Austin Macauley Publishers Ltd
25 Canada Square
Canary Wharf
London
E14 5LQ

Special thanks to Heather May Lancaster for her photographic genius and for David Jackson for supplying the equipment and pasties!

Part One
All the Tea in China...

Act One
Rainey's Day
1955 – New York City

The sidewalks and pavements were a hasty bustle of black umbrellas as the people of downtown New York City were rushing home to get out of the downpour of the worst rainstorm on record. The roads were jammed in gridlock as the early evening rush hour was in full swing. The bodies of the classic large American cars were gleaming and shining as the rain slanted out of a dark, bruised sky. He could hear the mass of horns blurting out in a mismatched tune as the many impatient drivers were blasting out their annoyance at the jam, all eager to make it home. Even though he was in a back alley to where the bustle and angry horn competition was taking place, he could hear the muffled shouts of the drivers swearing and arguing with each other.

He was slumped against a collection of metal trash cans, two of which had fallen over when he had collapsed against them, spilling the decayed remains of chicken bones and rotting vegetables over the back yard of the abandoned Chinese restaurant. His thick and sternly built body filled his police officers uniform snugly and he held his left shoulder with his large hand as blood ran through his fingers and over his officer's shield. His brass whistle had fallen from his lips and his .38 revolver laid in a loose grasp in his lap as he was soaked by the rain. His peaked officer hat had come off and lay at his feet as the rain wet his slick, black hair and broad, chiselled face, now showing the blue shadow of a man who had shaved early in the morning. He was looking at the tall figure that was lying face down in the rain some several feet away from him, the back of the figure's black trench coat was still gently letting the hot whispers of vapour from the three shots he had put in the body's back. Steam rose continually from the alleyway's vent system just a few feet away from the dead body, rising like a billowing cloud of white in the damp air.

It had been a long few months since the city had been haunted by the infamous Phantom, a killer that was not only thorough, but believed strongly in what they were doing. One unit of the New York Police Department was always dedicated to searching for the Phantom that specialised in killing the men of the numerous banks of the city.

Jasper Rainey was assigned to gather the statements from the housekeepers, servants and family members of the various bank managers to gather some sort of description of the killer, but no one saw or had heard a thing. The similarities of all the Phantom's victims were to be found in their beds with a deadly knife wound to the heart. The killer had also paused after their demise and very methodically cut a curved line either side of the men's faces, leaving them with a grotesque kind of smile. The killer had also taken the time to remove the victims' eyelids, leaving them forever staring at their bedroom ceilings, making it impossible for anyone to close their eyes.

It was the style of the killer that told Rainey that there were more to these acts than just murder. The time that the killer had taken after the fact to deface his victims told him a number of things. It told him that the killer was very patient and had some skill with a knife, such as a surgeon or artist. It also told him that the Phantom was not in a hurry and obviously had known where the other staff in the house would be that evening.

It also told him that the defacing was post mortem and that the intent was probably to hurt the families of the victims.

It was all too clear to Rainey that the killer was executing a very personal revenge.

The rest of the department would scoff at him and thought that it was obviously just another basket case that had a loan rejected from the bank. Rainey had pointed out that the targets had not worked within the same bank and that only a specific selection of the high rolling bankers who worked in central New York had been killed. These men didn't organise loans, they were responsible for running the entire banks. Their ridicule of him was so bad that he was struck off from the case and put back on his seat in downtown to deal with the junkies and small time gangsters that thrived in that part of the city. He had read in the morning paper that the Phantom had disappeared after the last killing and that they may never know who he was or why he had done the things he did.

Rainey knew that the killer had finished what he had set out to do and that now he just wanted to slip away and avoid being captured.

He had pursued the case in his spare time refusing to give up on the fact that one person could kill in such a manner and then just vanish. It was his lateral thinking that had led him down this path, taught to him by a man named Marvo. He had been very young when his mother had joined a ragtag group of travelling gypsies. She had fallen desperately in love with a dark eyed stranger from a travelling magic show as they had made their way across the Midwest. They stopped from town to town in their train of coloured, horse-drawn wagons to astound and amaze the locals with their intriguing gifts. There, every night the townsfolk would come and see the incredible feats of Marvo, the magician and his beautiful wife and assistant, Sophia. They would stand slack-jawed as he made her disappear in a glittering casket only to reappear at the back of the crowd wearing her sequined leotard and ostrich feather skull cap. The crowds would gasp in awe at the feats of strength displayed by Valorg, the Russian human bear, as he lifted a horse on his shoulders. The audiences swooned at Ikiru, the master of the orient, as time and again sticks shattered off of his impervious throat and they stared in wonder at the hot-shot Tex, as he ricocheted bullets off of tin plates mounted on the side to hit a bull's-eye with his single-action army revolver on a man sized paper cut-out. These were the attractions of Arkwright's circus of Magic and Imagination.

His mother took on the role of a fortune teller, a clairvoyant that could see the future and predict the coming of wealth and fertility to all those who sought it. He would sit quietly as a boy under her white linen clothed table, playing silently with his wooden car toys as he listened to her swoon the many customers who desired to know the future.

Marvo had told him that in life, just as in nature, all is not as it would seem. People will seek comfort in the fact that when a strong-willed person deemed that a danger had passed or that a mystery had been unveiled then they would be relieved because then things could go back to where they knew it was normal, to where it was safe. Marvo told him that in the animal kingdom such securities did not exist, that they all desired survival and would do unspeakable things to keep their world safe.

It was these very words that had struck a chord within Rainey as he went secretly through case files and eyewitness reports at the department. He had read that in all the victims' cases that they all had a man named Conrad Hartley in correspondence on their desks and files. Rainey knew of him of course, he was often in the papers pioneering for the abolishment of slavery, which still existed within the borders of America. He had also read that he had died of a heart attack at a goodwill dinner not so long back.

The Phantom had left no evidence behind as to his identity, no fingerprints, no forced entry into the bedrooms and no hair or other such physical evidence behind.

It was, however, the talcum powder that had given her away.

Sophia, who was wife and assistant to Marvo the Magnificent back in the days travelling with the circus, had often used talcum powder on her hands. When very young Jasper had asked her about it, she had explained that ladies of a certain status and dignity often used it to prevent chafing inside their occasional gloves.

Sophia had also admitted that she used it just before her knife throwing act, as it stopped her perspiring too much.

"He would be furious if I had missed," she had told him with a smile.

He had on many occasions, at the victims' homes, discovered traces of the powder on the carpets in the bedroom and sometimes on the pyjamas of the deceased. No forced entry or footprints on the grounds, to anyone outside it would appear to be an inside job, but they weren't looking for a girl, this was the work of a tall, brutal man. People had made up their own minds about what the Phantom had looked like and had come up with a Jack the Ripper type of bogeyman description; this was to give the killer some sort of identity and at least something to look out for, thus putting the public's mind at rest.

After much research, Rainey had discovered that the pioneer in question, Conrad Hartley had made a lot of enemies within the white community and even more so with the banks of New York. This was to pay their extremist groups off with large bribes so as not to start a fuss in southern America, where the banks' real interest lay.

Conrad's daughter was at his side the night he had been poisoned with an exotic cocktail of death at a goodwill feast in the name of freeing slavery. Although the papers never said, for it was much too distressing for the gentry of New York to bear, and Rainey had to go through the coroner's report to find out that Conrad had died on his bed with a hideous grin, unable to close his eyes. She was a struggling actress at the time and was familiar with makeup and props; she learned to walk on stunted stilts and applied for housekeeping jobs within the targets homes. Then she would watch and wait.

Rainey had followed her here to an abandoned theatre known as the Majestic where he had broken in and observed her many faces of disguise. She had caught him and a chase had begun with his overweight partner lagging behind, a chase that had ended in a shootout in this rain drenched alleyway.

He was losing consciousness as he saw his fat partner, Shamus Leary waddle hastily through the cloud of steam with his revolver drawn. His voice was a reverberated echo and a blur as Rainey passed out.

It was a month later when he was finally allowed to go home, he was taking large dosage of painkillers to relieve the searing fire in his shoulder where the bullet had pierced him. He sat in his apartment looking out over a closed courtyard, watching children play ball in the closed off atrium. He was holding a glass tumbler with orange juice over ice, he liked the way it jangled as he swirled it around, the taste of whiskey just a memory connected to that sound.

It had been a long two years since he had given the bottle up, a long struggle, which he wasn't sure he had the strength for. One glass just wasn't enough, the taste seemed to grab him and he wasn't satisfied until the bottle was empty. That was back when he and his wife had moved into a nice neighbourhood just outside the New York City limits. His little girl Carla, who was named after his mother, was only three years old then. His wife, Georgia, used to be a defence attorney for the state of Massachusetts but resigned her post when she had found out that she was pregnant. He had been transferred, here, to New York when the Dons and gangsters went to war with each other on the streets of New York. It was shortly after they had moved here that things started to go wrong. He was more and more absorbed with his work as one gangster in particular seemed to slip through the department's fingers, Beraldo Defranco. He was a real piece of work, rumours of him being connected to drugs, prostitution and even that he may have had a special studio where he had pictures taken of small children to sell to high rolling interested parties, were becoming stronger and stronger. The worst part about it all was that he had demanded from his lawyer police protection at all times as he had received many number of death threats, Rainey was among the officers' names selected to protect Defranco. It was driving Rainey mad, the routine of day in and day out of Defranco's scornful comments to him and his fellow officers. An unspoken innuendo that Defranco was not only getting away with it, but was being protected by the very force that was dying to bring him to justice.

Rainey's mood had blackened as the months wore on and his drinking became heavier, he was being eaten up from the inside and spent all his time at home shut away in his small den, going over news reports and old case files in the hope that he could find something, anything to pin on the smug Italian gangster. He promised himself that he wouldn't give him up. Not for all the tea in China. Georgia had tried to reason with him, to ease his mind and to try and make him see that he was losing his little girl, that she was at her wit's end and didn't know him anymore. The amount of whiskey he was drinking not only fired his temper but had unlocked the true nature of the beast and he had said things to her out of spite, things he had never said before, just to hurt her the way he was hurting.

There was no doubt in his mind that he had deserved it, when one day, he had come home from work to find a note on the living room table. He had been standing in the rain most of the day guarding the front of a high class restaurant, where Defranco was meeting with some friends. He even had the nerve to raise a large glass of wine through the window to Rainey with a huge smile as he ate an excellent lunch and his friends laughed at his gesture. Rainey knew what the note was going to say before he had read it. He had sat on the sofa and cried, his head bowed in shame and frustration.

Rainey joined the Alcoholic Rehab Programme through the Department's psychiatrist. At first he had agreed in the hope that he might win his wife's affections back, to somehow make up for the way he had treated her. She had told him over the phone that she was glad for him, but sternly told him that their marriage had come to an end. Rainey was crushed and had a couple of slips back into the bottle during his rehab until finally he grounded through it, taking to just drinking orange juice over ice in his whiskey glass, as a stark reminder of what that drink had done to his life.

Defranco's trial had been a lengthy one as the state prosecution had tried every trick in the book to put him behind bars. In the end, he had been cleared of all charges on a lack of substantial evidence and walked free, smiling on the court steps for the cameramen to snapshot it all over the next day's morning paper.

If Rainey could take one consolation from it was that at least he didn't have to babysit Defranco anymore, yet it still left a sour taste in his mouth. He had applied time and again for the position of Detective within the Department but had been rejected. He wasn't well liked at his station, the son of a woman who had laid and lived with gypsies, so this was no surprise to him. Being detective would grant him access to more sensitive materials regarding Defranco and so he kept applying after each rejection letter.

Today, however, was a little different, he held the brown envelope that he had picked up from the table whilst lost in reminiscing and turned it over in his hand. It was from the Chief Commissioner of police; all of his mail regarding police business usually came from the precinct, but this was entirely different.

He placed his drink down onto his plain, teak coffee table next to his pack of cigarettes and turned the envelope over in his large hands. His heart was beating hard as he tore it open and pulled out the clean, white paper.

'Dear Mr Rainey in view of your recent undeterred and sterling efforts in bringing a notorious and dangerous killer to justice, I hereby grant you the position of Detective, third class. Congratulations! Please report to your station for a debriefing and bring your badge and firearm with you.'

Rainey was smiling as he saw the Commissioner's signature at the bottom and he lowered the letter to his lap. "Finally!" he breathed. He was extremely happy, the kind of joy only hard work and patience brings.

"This calls for a proper celebration!" he lied to himself.

He stood up from the sofa and marched into the small dingy kitchen taking his glass with him. He emptied the orange juice and what was left of the ice into the grime-stained sink basin and then turned the tap on. The faucet groaned and whined and it shook with a loud rattling sound as the cold water came spluttering out and then settled into a steady run. He was humming tunelessly to himself as he rinsed his glass out. He turned the tap off and dried the outside briefly and then reached under the sink in a cabinet and fished a dusty bottle of whiskey that he had lodged at the back of the pipes. He didn't know why he had hidden it. It was not something that he could explain or justify. He had bought it the day he had to move out of the nice house in suburbia and into this cramped and rundown apartment in central. He took a handful of ice from the freezer and rattled them into his tumbler, still humming. He then moved back into the living room and sat as he broached the cork off the bottle with a crack. He was smiling as he poured the golden liquid over the ice, watching the cubes rupture and crack. He held the glass to his nose with his eyes closed inhaling the distinctive malty smell, and then opened his dark eyes looking at the wall in front of him.

He could hear the voices of those who had helped him in those two years: his fellow alcoholics, his tutors of the group, and the exercises they went through, the times he had sat in this very room shaking and gasping for just a glass, it was only one glass, he could stop after that, right? It was just one glass. But he hadn't, he had gone to the kitchen and had started frying eggs and bacon. Eating took away the need for drinking and he had survived another night without a drink, and a long stream of nights to follow.

He stood then, still with the whiskey in his hand, guilt washing through him like a rosy flush as he walked over to regard his reflection in one of the three objects he had salvaged from the love for his wife. The first was this mirror, he couldn't remember where it had come from—it was just a large oak framed mirror. He had propped it up on an old walnut sideboard and he remembered how she used to spend ages brushing her long, dark hair in front of it, humming sweetly to herself in her bathrobe. His eyes left his reflection to look at the small black and white photo of her, when she had made it through law school; she was dressed in the formal black robe with the mitre board style hat with a tassel. He remembered swelling with pride that day, oh how he loved her! The third was the most personal to him, it was a hairbrush. He had bought it at a Moroccan bazaar on their honeymoon; it was oval with a silver back and engraved with a fashionable symbol, surrounded by a polished wooden frame. She had used it that night before the party on the beach, other holiday makers were there and a roaring fire was lit. She had gotten more than a little tipsy and was dancing barefoot in front of him like a wild gypsy girl, holding up the sides of her hair as she made her body flow in front of him, holding his gaze with her smouldering eyes. The bonfire behind her had made her small white dress almost transparent and he watched with a smile as the silhouette of her long legs slipped this way and that, opening and closing to the music from the band on the beach. It had been the most perfect time of his life.

He had glassy eyes and a bittersweet smile on his chiselled face as he reached to pick up the hairbrush fondly.

His eyes went warm and there was a rush in his stomach, the room he was in dissolved away and his head felt like concrete. He was standing next to her in the old house, she was in the bedroom, and the steel grey light of dawn was slipping its long fingers through the blinds of the large bedroom window. She was dressed in her grey, pearl, silk negligee, amply showing her curves as she brushed her hair. In the background he could hear the sound of the running shower.

"Hey c'mon, you're going to be late! Any longer in there and you're going to shrink!" she said with a smile.

He tried to speak as he looked around their old bedroom, he was shaking, he could feel it but he knew he wasn't there. He looked down but couldn't see himself; he could hear himself chattering in a choking, stuttering voice as he watched her comb through her long hair. After a few moments he saw himself wearing a towel and his rippled, large frame swept up behind her with a smile as he watched himself kiss her neck.

"Let's not go to work! Let's go back to bed!" he swooned deeply to her. She laughed as she turned in his arms to kiss him.

"You old smoothie, you!" she laughed as she dropped the hairbrush onto the carpet.

There was a hollow rush in his ears as he felt his body pulled back through an invisible mass of sand and he was back in his room again, shaken and pale. He dropped the hairbrush and the whiskey on the floor as he fell back onto the arm of his sofa. The glass had smashed on the floor, as he was breathing hard, sweat rolling down his face. He could hear the sounds of the children outside and the cars passing in the street. He lifted his violently shaking hands up to his face in disbelief.

"What—what the hell is happening to me!" he stammered weakly.

Act Two
Penny Morgan

He didn't know how long he had sat there for, his hands palm up on his thighs. He was wearing his plain grey trousers and white shirt, opened at the throat. He was still slightly shaking and his dark eyes were still a little wild around the edges as he struggled with what had happened. His eyes moved around his grotty apartment and all the objects within, they stopped briefly on the candle stick, which was a family heirloom left in her will to him, when she had died four years earlier. It was a beautiful piece and really old, probably an antique. It was pearl white with angels standing back to back on the holder itself and the top was flared in a circle of intricate feathers, trimmed in gold. He then looked at the broken whiskey glass and his wife's hairbrush, still on the floor where they had fallen. His head was still reeling and if he was honest with himself, he was just too scared to touch anything else. He knew above everything else that he really needed a cigarette. His eyes flicked over to where his pack was on the table next to his wooden ashtray and matches.

"It was just stress that was all, I worked hard to track the Phantom and it was probably the shock of being shot," he told himself. He moved slowly and gingerly forward and reached with his fingertips over to the cigarettes. He took a breath and then patted them quickly, as if the pack had recently been hot and was scared he'd burn his fingers. He patted them again, slower this time and breathed a sigh of relief when nothing happened, "Just stress!" he smiled to himself and then picked the pack up shaking one free and struck a match on the heel of his black shoe. He leant back as he inhaled feeling much better. He was so much better that he felt confident to stand up from his couch and went to the kitchen to get a dustpan, he swept up the remains of his glass and put them in the trash. Picking the hairbrush up was a different story altogether, and he hovered over it for a while, just staring at it, before he summoned the courage to pick it up. He used his handkerchief from his pocket and carefully held it by the very end of its grip, treating it like a piece of evidence from a crime scene. He placed it gently back on the dresser and stepped back to observe his face in the mirror. His face had some colour back in it and his short stubble blackened his strong jaw, his eyes were still a little spooked and he decided a little fresh air was in order.

He grabbed his long grey overcoat from the peg by the door and secured his black trilby in place. Moments later he was walking down the steep staircase that folded back in on itself as he made his way from the top flight. The staircase had an old iron wrought, back to back, curved thorn bush-type design with a smooth wooden banister. Although it had been a bright sunny afternoon, the clouds that were gathering in the late summer sky were billowing dark grey as they swept in over Manhattan. He opened the double doors at the entrance to the long, broad steps leading down to the street. Sat on those steps were the familiar faces of some of the other residents of his block. These seven black guys from the streets of Brooklyn often sat outside, talking and whistling at any girl who walked by. Rainey knew them all by name and they all smiled at him as he walked out into the pale, late afternoon sun.

"Hey, Rainmaker! What's shaking?" The thin sinewy man with a purple leather cap asked him. He was alone at the top of the stairs with all his other friends on different steps below him, a status of rank in this neighbourhood.

"Hey, Stretch. You know, same old, same old," Rainey answered him.

"Word on the street says that you ain't going down well with your brothers in blue at the department," he said with his eyes lowered.

"Yeah well, that's what's called havin' a job, Stretch. You can't please everyone," Rainey said with a smile.

"Shute, man! If I gotta job who'd be out here on these steps makin' the neighbourhood look good?"

"Next time I'm in downtown, I'll ask your momma to take over for a while!" Rainey said with a smile. The thin black guy laughed, they double fist and Rainey went down the steps nodding to the other guys lounging there.

He made his way down towards Joe's bar only a few blocks from where he lived, the sights and sounds of his grimy street filling his nose, eyes and ears. He walked past his dusty, black car—a Cadillac Eldorado. It had seen better days, its long, wide front was street swept with dirty grime and the bodywork in general had dents and buckles in it. The rear left hub cap was missing and the windows were covered with the dusty breath of the city streets. The engine, though, was kept clean and ran well, a wolf in sheep's clothing. Rainey loved to be underestimated, it had proved useful time and again, and surprise had sometimes been the only weapon he had possessed.

He walked into the bustle of Joe's bar, a rowdy mismatched sound of men laughing, glasses clinking and waitresses in short flared black uniforms and white overall pinnies were shouting orders for food, whilst avoiding their backsides being pinched by the various men who were a little red-nosed as they leered at the girls black stockings. Smoke filled the air as the radio behind the bar played some fashionable jazz music. Joe was a short and twitchy kind of man. He spoke through his nose and he talked quickly, his nose had earned him the nickname, Needle. He was from Chicago and ended every other sentence with the word 'see'. He was an old friend of Rainey's from his whiskey days and had always made sure Rainey made it home. He smiled as he whipped down the bar to where Rainey had sat himself on one of the brown leather stools at the large, curved-bar.

"Hey Rainey," he said with a rat like smirk. "The usual?"

"Hey Joe, what's good?" Rainey replied as Joe settled himself.

"Ma's pie tonight is the bomb, see!" Joe said kissing his fingers.

"Ma's pie it is and no orange juice tonight, Joe."

Joe looked at him seriously then. "Hey, Rainey. I may be as dumb as a clam, but I ain't servin' you no whiskey, see!" he told him.

"Relax, Joe. I think I'm safe with a beer," the big detective told him. Joe seemed to relax and smiled again. "Comin' right up!" he said and scurried away.

He sat in a reflective mood as a barmaid placed a beer bottle on a napkin in front of him; he noticed that there were quite a few glasses that hadn't been cleared from the bar. The two sat next to him were identical in that they were club sodas and they had barely a sip out of them. The one nearest to him had a red lipstick mark around its rim. He thought of the many times his wife had done the exact same thing, the last time was at a café, downtown, after a fight and she had stormed out without finishing her coffee. She left nothing but a lipstick mark on her cup and a bitter taste in his mouth.

Beside the glass was an ashtray and a cigarette that had been half-smoked, its ashes had fallen from the lip in the tray onto the oak bar; it also had a lipstick mark on its filter. He pondered who the couple were, maybe a chance encounter with a friend or maybe something a little more intimate? Idly, he picked up the cigarette end to put it back in the ashtray.

It was more subtle this time, like a warming rush as his mind was pulled slowly through an invisible wall of sand, with a slow steady rush in his ears. It was also different this time, not as intrusive or as violent to his mind as it had been in his apartment, he was still aware of the noises and people around him, although he couldn't see them. What he was looking at was a woman. She was dressed a little upmarket for a joint like Joe's and wore a dark purple coat with a fox fur collar. A wide-brimmed, elegant hat of the same colour was perched at an angle on her flowing dark brunette hair. A see-through veil with black sparkled sequins covered her eyes as she smoked the long white cigarette with a gold filter that he had picked up from the bar. She sat next to a man who had

25

ordered a club soda; he was dressed just as elegantly as she was in a black silk waistcoat with a gold pocket watch tucked in, secured with a gold chain. His coat was matching, the kind of coat that a gentlemen would wear to a fashionable occasion, not to a downtown bar in Lower East Side. It was his face, though, that confused Rainey as he observed his vision. He couldn't see it; it was just a rippled blur, as if it wasn't his real face, almost as if he was wearing some kind of mask that his sight couldn't penetrate. In his top left hand button hole he wore a single white flower—a lily.

When the barmaid asked the lady what she would like to have, she didn't answer, she just pointed at the drink that the gentleman had ordered. They just sat there side by side on their stools, not talking, not even looking at each other, as the barmaid brought her the club soda with a napkin beneath it. Just then a group of four rowdy men burst through Joe's doors, they were laughing and jeering as a couple of them were pushing each other playfully on the shoulder. They moved past the couple and made their way to the right of the curved-bar where they loudly ordered their drinks. She sat for a moment looking around the bar as the man pulled a gold cigarette case from his waistcoat and lit a slender cigar. She then picked her drink up, her cigarette still between her fingers, and took a sip, then put the glass down next to the napkin. She then opened a small chic, black purse that shimmered the same way her veil did and pulled out a small compact. She then popped it open and seemed to regard her lipstick. Rainey, however, saw her pull a small pencil from the purse with the other hand and scribbled something on her napkin without even looking at what she was doing. The man with the white flower smoothly placed his drink upon it and then slid it over in front of him. She then placed both the pencil and the compact back in her purse and took another draw from her cigarette, then stubbed it in the ashtray as she stood to leave.

Rainey's mind was pulled gently back through that invisible wall of sand and he was sat at the bar still holding her gold tipped cigarette. He wasn't as startled this time, the feeling of coming back from his vision had been warming, even comforting. He looked about the bar to see if anyone had noticed him looking weird whilst he had been in his vision, but they were still drinking and talking as normal. He looked to the right of the bar where the four men who had come in were still jeering and shouting at each other in high spirits. He noticed that they were all halfway through their second round of beers.

"That couple was just in here! I must have just missed them," he mumbled deeply to himself. He then wondered what it all meant, this was obviously some kind of exchange, but what was being exchanged? What did she write on that napkin and why would two well-dressed people come here? If this was a secret rendezvous then someone would remember their clothes, they stuck out like sore thumbs in the crowd of people wearing grey workingman's caps and cheap dresses. It didn't make any sense. His thoughts were interrupted by a young girl who was making her way around the bar; she was emptying all the large ashtrays into a tin bucket. He looked down at his ashtray as he placed her stump carefully in his coat pocket and clearly saw a vision of the man with the flower and thin cigar. He quickly pulled a cigarette from his soft pack, as she approached him. They both reached for the ashtray, at either end, as he stopped her.

"Come back for this one, OK honey? It would be a shame to mess up a new one, just for one smoke," he said with a smile, his cigarette pitching in his mouth as he spoke.

"Awww, you're so sweet Rainey, thanks. If only all the bums in here were as thoughtful as you," she said warmly and then made her way around the rest of the bar.

He watched her go then took his smoke out of his mouth and put it on the bar. He then turned his attention to the cigar in the ashtray, and took a breath. "OK, let's see if this works." he mumbled without much enthusiasm. He sat for a moment looking at the half smoked cigar, whilst flexing his big hands above it in anticipation of what might happen when he touched it. He reached down and gingerly picked the cigar from the tray.

One rushing wall of sand later, he was watching the blurred faced gentleman sitting at the bar, as she left without saying a word. Although Rainey couldn't see himself, he felt as though he could move around within the area of the well-dressed gentleman. He couldn't explain how, it was like an out of body experience looking back into the past, like being in the re-run of an old show, without actually being there. He was looking over the man's shoulder as he very slightly moved the glass to look at her napkin. It read, "WM 5705."

A phone number? Rainey thought, his own voice in his head slightly echoing. *Maybe I've got this all wrong! Maybe the reason they were in here was because people of their class wouldn't be seen dead in here! It could be that she had to slip him her number so that they could arrange a more intimate meeting.*

The man then took a sip of his drink and placed it on his own napkin, whilst slipping hers into his pocket. He then placed his cigar in his mouth and stood to make his way to the restroom at the far left of the bar. Rainey followed, with the weird sensation of moving without his legs. He entered and went to the last stall with a notice that read, 'out of order'. He opened the door and stood inside. Rainey watched as he wrote in pencil WM 5705 on the stall wall; next to some very explicit drawings and rude jokes that someone else had written. He then left back for the bar, took another short draw from his cigar and then stubbed it in the ashtray.

Rainey was back in the real world and sat holding the stump of the cigar in his fingers, rolling it around, lost in thought. "How very strange!" He mused as Joe came from the other end with his meal; he slipped the cigar into his other pocket and smiled as Joe neared him.

"Best pie in the city, see? Ma says you need any extra, it's on the house! Said you're looking a little peaky, see!" Joe told him.

"You tell your ma, she's a lady in a million," Rainey said gratefully.

By the time he had finished his meal and talked to Joe awhile, the kind of thankful small talk that people often made when they had been looked after at a dinner of a friend's house. It was getting late, darkness had blanketed New York and the nightfall had brought another downpour. He stood at Joe's doorway and buttoned his long coat, turning his collar up and pulled the peak of his black hat down a little. The rain wreathed out of the sky and hissed on the slick tarmac of the road, the pavement was shiny and reflected the red sign above the doorway, 'Joe's Bar'. The cars that were parked in the street and that passed along the road were gleaming in the downpour, the streetlamps' light slipping over their bodywork. He made his way home slowly, his shoes striking smartly on the wet concrete as Ma's pie sat solidly in his stomach, insulating him against the wind.

He was lost in thought about what he had seen at the bar. Unsure of where and why this peculiar gift of vision had come from. He wondered if there was something wrong with him, if the bullet that the Phantom had shot him with had somehow poisoned his body, giving him a rare form of cancer or a bleed in the brain, making him see things that weren't actually there. He wrestled with it not sure what it meant or if what was happening to him was permanent or just a temporary thing. Whatever the case, it was showing him something, a truth that other people couldn't see. His mind wandered back to the faceless gentleman at the bar, why had he written that woman's phone number on the stall in the men's bathroom? That didn't make sense to him at all and it felt rather sinister to him, like he was missing a piece of a very large puzzle.

His thoughts were shattered by a woman's voice calling out to him from the corner of the street he lived down.

"Hey, handsome! How about a smoke for a good time gal?" she giggled.

He looked up to where she had called out to him and smiled at her as he crossed the rain swept street. Her name was Penny Morgan a hooker from Lower West Side. Normally, she would work the patch her pimp had given her, who was a fair kind of guy from New Orleans and treated his girls right. Unlike Penny's last pimp, who used to beat her in order to get more money and work out of her, until Rainey had paid him a visit. Tonight though, she was here for a different reason. She was a pretty thing, a natural beauty, who wore too much make-up in Rainey's opinion. She wore her familiar white short dress and red sweater along with slightly tarnished stockings, the rips through which her thighs showed; she looked cold and damp as she shrunk underneath her small pink umbrella.

"Hey there, Honey," he said warmly as he came over to her standing next to an alley that separated each apartment block in the street. He pulled a cigarette out and lit it for her, as she stood shivering in the rain. "It's a little damp tonight for you, isn't it?"

"Rain doesn't stop the rent bein' paid, handsome! Care to help me out? I'll keep you warm all the way home!" she said with a smouldering look of her blue eyes. He nodded at her with a smile and she took him by the hand, down into the alleyway, the torrent of rain washing in streams down the mossy brickwork from unseen broken gutters above them. He stood with his back against one of the drier places in the alley and bent forward as she brought her face up to the side of his cheek, she didn't touch him and neither did he touch her, but it looked to anyone passing by that they were kissing each other's necks.

"What's new?" he whispered in her ear.

"The man I was with last night was boasting about some kind of job here in New York, said his friends were coming to lighten the load of the New York Bank. He said, it was going to be smooth and that he was going to make more money than he could spend. He said, he was coming back on Thursday to marry me."

"Is that a normal thing they say?" Rainey asked her, slightly amused.

"Oh, you have no idea!" she whispered with a sigh. Rainey smiled at that.

"Did he say where they were coming from? What crew would be pulling it off?" he whispered.

"He said, they were coming from Washington and that something had to be done about staying on the Viper's territory. He did say that the House of Cards would be smoothing the job. But I've never heard of them."

"So the bank job will be this week, it's Monday tomorrow and that gives me four days to find out when it will actually take place. Well done Penny, but as a personal favour to me, please stay safe! If things start to get dicey, I want you to cut and run for Joe's, OK?"

"Deal," she agreed. "I'd better get going, I'll be in touch. What'll it be, the usual?"

"Sure," he said smiling as he slipped fifty dollars into her hand.

She then stood up sharply, away from him, with a look of disgust on her face and shouted at him. "How dare you, you filthy old man!" She then stormed towards the street and out into the rain, he followed her out and she turned sharply around.

"I told you I'm not doing that, you filthy monster!" she fumed at him.

"But honey, I thought you were that kind of girl!" he protested.

She slapped him hard around the face as she stormed off down the street into the curtain of rain, as he stood there holding his cheek with a smile. "Take care of yourself, Penny Morgan," he said softly, and then turned to walk back to his apartment block, under the watchful gaze of the many elderly women who stood at their windows scowling at him.

Act Three
Just Like Magic

The next morning, he rose early from a night of twisted and bizarre dreams. Dreams of faceless men and of his wife dancing in front of him dressed in a dark purple coat with a fox fur and veil across her eyes, her hands running free with blood. He sat at the side of his bed in his white long johns and vest, his large frame breathing slowly with his head bowed and his hands on his thick thighs. The images of his dreams were still vivid and coursed through his memory. It was still fairly dark outside and only the slightest hue of grey was staining the sky, as the rain still fell relentlessly against his window pane. The questions that he had been asking himself, yesterday, were starting to swarm his mind, like a gathering of angry hornets. The first thing he was going to do at the precinct today was try the number that the faceless man had written on the bathroom stall. Maybe then he could start getting some answers to the nature of the bizarre meeting at Joe's bar. Even though, there was nothing there to say they had done anything wrong, he had a strong feeling in his gut that it was all rather sinister and was the start of something quite evil. He couldn't explain why, it was just a feeling and more often than not, he had found that the first feeling was always the correct one.

He wiped his large palms down the front of his face and stood to get ready for his first day as a detective. He moved through to the small bathroom and turned the taps with the shower hose attached. The pipes rattled and knocked in a shrieking complaint, as the water coughed and spluttered from the metal showerhead. He knew it would take a while for the hot water to come through, so he went back to the bedroom and opened the top drawer of his wooden bureau.

He fished around various bits and pieces of memorabilia that he and his wife had collected over the years. The champagne cork from their first new year together, scattered loose pictures of him and his daughter together, which he had promised himself he would put in frames one day, trinkets and souvenirs that they had got on their holidays together. They were meaningless to anyone else, but to Rainey they were priceless.

At the bottom of the drawer he found what he was looking for, his old service .45 automatic handgun. It was military issued, black with a dark brown wooden side grip; it held seven rounds and was more potent than his issued .38 revolver. It wasn't loaded and he turned it around in his hand, feeling the weight again, after so long. The small brass plaque on the grip read 'Lady Luck'. It wasn't chrome plated with a pearl handle like the one that hot-shot Tex had given him for his eighteenth birthday, a trick shot automatic that Tex had incorporated into his show at one time. It had been bored out and fitted with a special receiver, making it a real nail driver.

Tex used to amaze the crowds as he shot it through a thick sheet of wood, a thick sheet of stone and finally a sheet of mild steel, to finally hit an apple on a spike at the far end.

His service in the US Military had been short lived, just three years to be exact. He was a young man when he had been drafted and was assigned as a Colonel's aide. He wanted to serve his country out in the field like all the young men at the time, with passion in their hearts and a fire in their belly. Unfortunately, not for Rainey, his day to day routine in the military was bringing the Colonel his breakfast, morning paper and coffee. As the months went on, Rainey noticed a steady stream of young boys visiting the Colonel. At first he thought they were family, nephews and friends of nephews. One night he was called from by the Commander to get the Colonel for a matter of state importance. When Rainey entered the room, the military Colonel was dressed in high heels and suspenders complete with basque, he was flaying a naked 12 year old boy with a whip and berating him like a mother, complete with voice and tone. Rainey ran over and punched him hard, knocking the man out and then put one of the Colonel's coats over the boy and lead him out of the room.

There was no trial, no inquest as to what had happened, Rainey spent two weeks in the brig and then was dishonourably discharged, and that was his military career over with. He smiled as he remembered hitting that overweight piece of trash and then looked inside the drawer for the three ammunition clips, he had for it, and the box of bullets. Under the white and red box, he saw something that took his breath away. It was his mother's brooch, fashioned in metal and colours with a sparkling sheen in the shape of a cuckoo. His mother had been raised in a woodland cattle ranch in Middle America. She would tell him sometimes when she and her father would stop for lunch, they would sit beneath the shade of tall, dark spruce trees and listen to the haunting sound of the cuckoos' talking. Rainey shrunk back from the drawer, petrified to touch the brooch. He closed the drawer slowly holding the box of bullets in his other hand.

He sat on his bed feeding the brass cased bullets into the top of the clips. He was lost in thought as he heard them slip in, one by one. Finally, when they were all loaded, he clipped them into the belt of his military gun holster and then slipped the first magazine into the gun, he pulled the slide back and then let it snap forward, the weapon was now ready to fire.

He slipped the colt into his holster and left the bedroom to shower.

It was a very wet drive to Precinct 15; the wipers of his Eldorado swiped the downpour away as he sat behind the wheel of the heavily growling engine. He had his window rolled down a little as he smoked a cigarette, listening to a New York radio station playing a Frank Sinatra tune. The car smoothly moved down the slick street leaving a throaty gutter sound in its wake. He was ready for them, he knew the looks he would get from the other detectives there, that scornful whisper of a man, who did not belong in their ranks. Fortunately, most of them would be polite to hold their tongue and keep their opinions inside their heads; Rainey was after all, a very big man.

Precinct 15 was a squat, ugly looking building, quite large compared to other precincts and was situated in Lower East Side. It was here that the boys in blue had to deal with at least 1500 cases a day, lost people, lost pets, domestic violence, stolen vehicles, rape and murder. These were just some of the cases that the men and women of Precinct 15 came face to face with, the moment they entered the building, in 15 there was no such word as 'lunch'.

He swept on past the parking lot where he would normally park and drove around to the underground garage where the detectives parked, and where the mechanics saw to the maintenance of the squad cars. His tyres squealed a little as he rumbled up to the automatic red and white barrier to the sloped concrete ramp down into the garage. After a moment, the barrier raised up and the black car slipped in out of the rain, just inside was another barrier and a tall man wearing a denim dungaree stood behind it with his greased arms folded. Behind him in columns to the left and right were the parked black and white squad cars and behind them was the bay where the detectives parked. The Eldorado's engine growled and grumbled louder in here, echoing off of the concrete surroundings. The man in the dungaree's walked slowly round to the driver's window, staring harshly at Rainey.

"You lost Rainey?" he said sarcastically.

"Yeah, McKenzie, I was on my way to your momma's house and took a wrong turn," he replied.

"Who taught you that line? You're gypsy momma? Bet she was real good at visiting houses!" McKenzie sneered.

"Yeah, she would have done it…if your dad hadn't beaten her too it." Rainey said calmly. McKenzie looked angry and started to move around the barrier to his car. Rainey opened the door and swung out, towering over the slim man, his dark eyes intent.

"You got something else to say about my momma or is the next place you are visiting going to be New York Central Hospital?" he growled.

McKenzie stepped back a bit as the big man swung out of his car and didn't look so sure, but still held his ground. "You can smart mouth me all you want, Rainey, but you ain't parking that piece of crap in here! It's for detectives only! Not for flat foots! Are you getting the picture?" he barked at him.

"I'll remember you said that, why don't you call upstairs and ask what I'm doing here?" Rainey told him as he sat on the bonnet of his car, the engine still throbbing deeply.

"Don't think I won't!" McKenzie retorted as he stormed off toward his booth and the black telephone inside. Rainey could see him talking to himself darkly, as he spun the dial on the phone in his booth, cradling the hand set in his neck. Rainey sat quite comfortably on the front of the car as he smoked his cigarette, watching McKenzie's face contort from disbelief into complaint and then finally into shameful resignation as the voice on the other end told him of Rainey's new status in the department. After a moment he came out with a strained face, it looked like his face was on fire.

"It really are these little victories that bring such joy to life," Rainey said satisfactorily as the tall man silently opened the barrier. He returned to sit behind the steering wheel and slammed his car door with an echoed boom, then slid the car up slowly to stop and look at McKenzie through his open window. "I want a shotgun grip fitted in this car before this afternoon! I'd hate to have to report you on my first day as a detective!" Rainey told him sternly. "Are you getting the picture?" He then drove into the bay slowly glaring at the tall man as he slipped on by.

Rainey's commanding officer was a dumpy, fairly short, angry looking man. His cheeks always seemed to be flushed a shiny red colour, matching his ever-increasing bald patch on the crown of his head. His name was Albert Sharpe and he had been at this position longer than he would care to remember. He had always dreamed of having a position with the FBI, but it was here where his career had peaked and he had been rejected any number of times by the agency. It was this repeated rejection, more than anything, that had created his sour disposition, that and an increasingly demanding wife, an irritable bowel and high blood pressure. It was the story of every detective that worked here on the second floor; your day just wasn't complete unless you had a chewing out from Sharpe.

Rainey was still a half hour early when he walked through the double doors to the bustling Homicide Division. It was a long room, lined either side with rows of wooden desks that bore black imperial typewriters and black telephones with switchboard buttons on them. Right at the far end, past the rows of concrete pillars that ran as supports for the building was Sharpe's office. It was closed in with a large window at its front, so that everyone could witness him storming away at whatever poor soul had been unfortunate enough to stray into his crosshairs. Sharpe was standing in front of his office with an unlit half cigar jammed in his mouth with two women on either side showing him report files. His would glance at one then turned to glance at the other, nodding to himself. He looked up as Rainey approached him.

"Alright keep me posted on this one!" he growled at the girl on the left as he jabbed her file with a stubby finger. "Now shoo!" he snapped.

The two women quickly melted away into the busy throng of people who were moving about the office, as the air was filled with mumbled voices on the telephone and the sound of still ringing ones. He looked Rainey up and down as he rolled his cigar in his thin lipped mouth.

"You're late, Rainey!" he growled.

"I had a little trouble parking," he replied smoothly.

Sharpe grunted. "Is that a fact?" He then turned and opened the wooden door to his office. "Let's get this over with!" He grated. The big man followed Sharpe into his office closing the door, sealing the ringing chaos outside to a mere murmur. The dumpy man straightened the front of his brown waistcoat as he sat in his large black leather chair, a match and lit his cigar. He reached into a drawer and brought out a gold detective's badge, which Rainey took, placing his old silver shield into Sharpe's stubby hand. "You can keep your .38 most guys carry a backup," he told him, disgruntled.

"Let's be straight Rainey," he said in his growling whiskey voice as he leaned back in his creaking chair. "I didn't want you here. Frankly, I am amazed at the Commissioner's decision to make you a detective after you got lucky getting on the trail of that Phantom character. The only reason you are here is because I got over ruled. Don't get me wrong, I'm sure you put in the hours to try and track that nutball down, I just expect to see the same dedication here. The assignments that come across your desk will be the ones that the real detectives in here don't have time to deal with."

"I'll do my best not to disappoint, Chief," Rainey said in a mildly sour tone.

"Oh, by all means, do! The moment you mess up, I'll be happy to load your ass in a sling and launch you back downstairs to the flat foots," he told him with a crooked smile. "Any questions before Sandra show's you to your desk?" he added still smirking.

"Just one," Rainey replied as he turned to stand at the door. "Whatever happened to brothers in unity, uniting to protect this city and her interests for the good of the common people?"

"Where on earth did you read that drivel?" Sharpe laughed a barking sound.

"It's on the plaque the Commissioner gave you in the picture behind you," Rainey said smirking, and then left the office leaving Sharpe to turn quickly in his chair to look at his prized framed photo.

He met Sandra outside the office, where she stood smiling.

"I don't know what you said to him, but anything that takes that smug smile off his face makes my day." She chuckled, then took him over to a large desk that had his name plaque on it and an already half full in tray of folders and papers. There were four other detectives who stood around a desk in the central isle, one was sitting on its corner as the rest of them were trying hard not to laugh, while giving him brief sidelong looks and whispering to each other.

"Don't pay them any attention; they all think they're tough guys. The real top dog of this department, the one in the blue shirt, is the Commissioner's youngest son. So, he gets treated differently from the rest of us," Sandra told him.

"Thanks," he said gratefully.

"Coffee is over there, restroom is over there. No doubt you'll be seeing a lot of both of them. Welcome to 15, Detective Rainey," she said and then walked back up the aisle to her desk.

The first thing he did as he hung his long grey coat on the back of his chair was reach for the phone. He picked up the receiver and after a moment a female voice said, "Operator."

"Yes, Operator, could you give me New York 5705, please?" he asked her. She patched him through and the phone was rang. After a moment a woman answered in a very crisp but friendly fashion.

"Good morning, Silk and Satin, how can I help you?"

"Yes, good morning, I was just wondering what is it that you do there?" Rainey replied a little confused.

"We are the largest manufacturer of personalised toiletries and bathrobe's for the majority of New York's many prestigious hotels, sir. We hand-stitch bath towels, face cloths and many items in whatever the hotel's name may be. We also…"

She was still telling him the inventory of what the company personalised and what the going rate was for their services and all he was thought was that this was a dead end. "Thank you I'll be in touch!" He interrupted her and then put the phone down. It didn't make any sense at all if the letters and numbers she had given him were not a phone number, and then what else could they mean? It would have to wait for now as his attention turned back to the mass of paper and folders that sat in his in tray.

Sharpe had been true to his word about his case load, as Rainey sifted through the grey and blue folders. It took him most of the day to go through all of them and it was late afternoon before he was able to start marking them in order of importance. They were missing persons for the most part, quite old cases but not too old as to people still calling to see if there was any progress or sightings of them. The rest were unsolved murders, amongst the many homeless and prostitute communities. These were not the sort of things that the cool kids of the department could be bothered with, so they had dumped them on Rainey's desk. There was one case in particular that had caught his attention and even made him raise an eyebrow. It was the brutal murder of a downtown prostitute, some five years ago. She was unnamed and never identified and it looked as though it was some sort of revenge killing. The photos he looked at showed that Jane Doe had been shot in the face with a shotgun, then scorched by a blowtorch along her forearms and hands before finally being thrown into the sea. She had washed up bloated and unrecognisable on a small beach by the New York Harbour and found by a group of kids who were down there skipping stones.

"What a way to go!" he murmured to himself. Just then his phone erupted into a loud ring, making the hairs on his neck stand on end. He picked it up quickly.

"Detective Rainey, Homicide," he said in a clear voice.

"Hey Detective, the boys on the beat found a body at the back of Washington and Maine 57th Street," the girl at the switchboard told him.

"OK thanks, tell them I'm on my way," he replied and swept out of his chair, grabbing his coat and hat. As he left he heard one of the four guys that were sniggering at him before call out. "Go get 'em, Champ!" he said as they all burst out laughing.

Rainey gritted his teeth as he made his way down to the motor pool.

McKenzie had done as he was told and fitted the shotgun lock to the dash of his car, complete with a Remington pump action. He had also fitted a standard police band two way radio. Rainey gave him a nod of thanks as he drove out of the underground garage, back into the curtain of rain. The drive downtown was hectic as the roads were pretty gridlocked, Rainey had to place his magnetic red light on his roof and send it spinning to clear his way to 57th Street. When he got there, a bunch of officers had blocked the road off, dressed in waterproof cowls over their uniforms. They opened their barrier and Rainey parked his Eldorado in the middle of the deserted street, surrounded by the swirling red lights of the many black and white squad cars.

He climbed out into the hissing deluge as a policeman walked up to the car shielding his face against the rain.

"Detective Rainey? I'm officer Sam Peters this way, sir," he smiled.

"Do we have anything on the victim?" Rainey asked, as they made their way through the rainfall.

"His name's David Ellis, he had just got a job working the docks by the Hudson, single guy, no relatives. That's all we have so far, Detective," Sam replied.

He led him from the main street into a litter-strewn back adjoining alley. The back windows of all the apartments looked at each other from across the alley, where the base of the fire escapes were packed with rubbish sacks, piled for the trash men the next morning. In an alcove at the top of the alley and buried beneath many of those sacks was a dead young man. Rainey turned to Sam with the rain streaming off of the peak of his cap.

"Keep those people back, Sam, and no reporters yet, OK?" he said. Sam nodded and walked away as he started to relay orders to the other officers, and for a moment Rainey was alone with the pale faced man. Rainey noticed that David Ellis was in his mid-twenties and quite athletic, dressed in long johns with a knife wound to the heart, quick and clean. It was a strange thing to be wandering around in your underwear and Rainey wondered if the killer had removed them after the act, or if they had been stolen by the various tramps that hung around this area. He took a deep breath and looked around as he checked he wasn't being watched. "Alright, let's see who you were, my friend," he murmured as he took the dead man's hand.

There was no gentle rush this time, his head was filled with impassable concrete and an unearthly whistling shout, it shouted beyond a hollow wall, screaming at him as his body started to flood with a powerful icy chill, he barely managed to let go as the chill flowed through him, holding his fingers to the man's dead skin. He pulled back with all his strength and fell back onto the wet ground on his back side, breathing hard. It took a couple of minutes to regain his breath and when he did he said to himself, "Maybe not! Let's not do that again!" There were clearly limitations to his new found gift.

He stood shakily from the slumped body and steeled himself; he would never forget that unexplainable feeling of coldness and loss, a feeling that would haunt him for the rest of his life. He looked up then at the rain soaked alley, just in time to see a little girl quickly swipe the curtains closed as Sam walked back up to him. "Sam have you got any witnesses in the neighbourhood?"

"None that are coming forward, Detective," he told him.

"OK, give me a minute, Sam," he said as he made his way to the apartment's backdoor steps, where he had seen the little girl. He made his way up the slick stone steps and rang on the startling electric bell that reverberated from within. He pulled his collar up as the rain soaked his shoulders and the back of his coat. After a couple of minutes, a man dressed in trousers and a deep red dressing gown came to open the door.

"Hey, I'm Detective Rainey. May I have a few moments of your time please, sir?"

The man looked a little hesitant but nodded and beckoned him in. Rainey nodded his thanks as he stepped in from the rain onto the small black and white tile floor. The rain was running from the brim on his hat as he addressed the man. "We are just doing some routine enquires, sir. If it would be OK, I might have a word with your daughter?"

"My daughter didn't see anything," he said defensively.

"I'm sure she didn't, sir, but like I said we are just following up on routine enquires," he assured him.

"Are you OK, Detective? You look like you've seen a ghost," the man asked looking into his dark eyes.

"Damn weather goes right through you," he said with a thin smile. "May I?" he continued pointing up the stairs.

Rainey walked up the stairs and took his hat off and smoothed his hair with his hand as he knocked politely on the pink-peeled bedroom door. There was no answer so he eased his way in to regard an empty bedroom full of stitched toys and homemade mobiles and a ceiling of glittering moons and stars. He went straight for the oak double door wardrobe at the left of the room and once again knocked politely.

"Go away, I'm not here!" a girl's muffled reply came.

"Of course, you're not! If you were here but not there, everyone would know where to find you!" he said as he sat on his heels. "My name's Jasper. What's yours?"

"Emily," she said shyly from within the wardrobe.

He opened the door and smiled at her as she cowered beneath her collection of hand-me-down dresses and coats. "Now this is a neat hiding place," he said looking around her closet.

"Are you going to take me to jail?" she asked, a little terrified.

"No, Emily. I just want to ask you a few questions, OK?" She nodded slowly. "Do you often look out of your window at night?"

"I sometimes have bad dreams and I can't sleep so I look out the window till I'm tired again."

"Very clever! I must remember that one the next time I have a bad dream." He smiled. "Did you see anything unusual last night, honey? It's OK, you can tell me, I'm a police detective."

"How do I know that you won't arrest me when I tell you?"

Now he was in no doubt that Emily had seen something and would have to do something above the ordinary to win her confidence. He reached into his pocket and pulled out a shiny quarter. "Everyone sometimes tells lies, Emily, but I've found only this tells the truth. You wanna see a magic trick?"

She nodded with her lips inverted.

He stood and went over and picked up a small glass tumbler, stained with her handprint on the bedroom side cabinet. He then placed it on the floor in front of the cupboard, where she was hiding. He placed it cup side up on the carpet in front of her with the shiny coin in his fingers. "OK, this is how it works. Mystery takes the coin away. Truth brings it back. If you want to keep the quarter, you must tell the truth, OK?"

She nodded as she edged forward to look at the glass upturned on the floor.

"OK, watch carefully," he said as he breathed in sharply and then released his breath dramatically. He placed the quarter in his open palm and then closed it. After a moment he opened them both and they were both empty. "What did you see last night at your window?" he asked still holding his hands in the air above the empty glass.

"There was a man talking to another man, one man was wearing a jacket with a snake on it and the other was wearing a white flower in his pocket."

"A white flower? Like a lily?" Rainey asked.

"Yes, like a lily. They were all over my mom's coffin, when they buried her."

He held her hands then and looked at her. "Can you tell me what the man with the flower looked like Emily?" he said softly.

"He had a very sharp beard and his eyes were very black and twinkly. His face looked like it hadn't seen the sun in a long time. He was talking to the man with the snake on his jacket and told him, 'well done'."

"What time did you see this?" he asked.

"I don't know it was early. Is the nice man from number five dead?" she asked then.

"Yes Emily, I'm afraid so. But I'm sure your mom is looking after him, honey!"

He thought for a moment before standing as his mind raced.

"Hey, you said the truth would bring the quarter back!" she said pointing at the empty glass on the floor.

He smiled then said, "So I did, little lady." He then snapped both his fingers and the glass suddenly tinkled and shook as if something had fallen inside it. She squealed with delight and quickly picked the glass up; on the carpet was the shiny quarter he had made disappear.

She gasped in awe as she picked it up. "Just like magic!" she whispered.

"Just like magic." He laughed.

"Thank you, Jasper!" she said gratefully.

"No thank you, Emily," he said as he walked down the stairs and back into the rain.

Part Two

Act Four
Johnny Snakebite

It was late evening when he had finished typing his report up at the station and only him and the night staff of the precinct were still in the building. He stopped and rubbed his tired eyes and then stretched. His stomach rolled and yawned as it reminded him that he had missed lunch. He decided that a stop off at Joe's might be in order and maybe a slice or two of Ma's pie. The drive to Joe's was reflective as he rumbled through the shining wet city streets. The rain had stopped for now, leaving only a black mirrored glow on the floor of the many electric signs that still buzzed and shone onto the tarmac's slick surface. It was late and well past half seven when he pulled up outside Joe's bar. He entered the cosy, warm place with the usual rowdy rabble who sat drinking and laughing. Joe was talking to a customer when he saw Rainey and made his way over to the end of the bar where Rainey sat. They exchanged the usual pleasantries and he ordered Ma's pie again. During their conversation he asked Joe a question.

"Hey Joe, what's wrong with your toilet in the men's restroom?"

"Nothing. It sometimes gurgles a lot but apart from that it's as clean as a whistle, see?"

Rainey knew that he had absolutely no idea about the 'out of order' sign that had been placed there previously. When he had finished his meal, he went to the stall at the end in the restroom. He scanned the inside of the wall and saw that the previous WM 5705 had been erased and underneath a new number had been written. WM 5621. His brow creased in confusion, the letters and numbers that had been written were not even in the same handwriting. In fact, they looked like they had been written by a child. Maybe just a child's prank to deface the original? Or was it something more? Rainey left the restroom and checked the ashtray on his way to say goodbye to Joe. There were nothing but standard butt-ends and he decided to make Joe aware of the high-class dressed man and woman who had been in his bar the previous night.

Joe was rapidly scrubbing a cloth over his bar top as Rainey approached him.

"Hey, Joe, be sure to thank Ma for the pie, I'm heading for home now," he told him with a warm smile.

"Sure, Rainey, I'll tell her, see?" Joe replied, not looking up from his frantic cleaning.

"There was a man and woman in here earlier, not your average customers. Did you happen to notice them?"

"Yeah, yeah, I remember them, Mr straight suit and Mrs Florence Nightingale; guess Ma's pie is attracting high rollers to the joint, see?"

Rainey laughed. "It's good enough for royalty, Joe," he assured him. "Listen, if they happen to come back, will you be a pal and let me know?"

"Sure, Rainey, if I see them, I'll tell you I saw them, see?"

The big man was smiling at Joe as he put his hat back on, the smile of a man who was aware of his friend's unaware play on words. Joe looked up, then sensed Rainey was still waiting on something.

"What is it, Rainey? I got work going on here, see?" he said sharply.

"Nothing, Joe, thanks again," he said as he went to push his way through the door into the night air. "I'll see you later, see?"

Joe watched him go as he left chuckling to himself with a needle-nosed hard stare.

"Wise guy!" he muttered to himself and then carried on assaulting the bar top with his cloth.

When he got to his apartment, he stopped at his door, there was light coming from underneath it and he never left the light on all day. He slipped his gun from the holster and slowly turned the handle. He swiftly moved in with his .45 automatic at the ready. He came face to face with Penny Morgan, who was sitting on his sofa with tears streaming down her cheeks and a large bruise on her face. He lowered his firearm and closed the door.

"Who did this Penny?" he asked.

"It was a man from Washington." She sniffed. "They call him Toledo. His friends are planning something in the city, it has something to do with the bank, and he thought I might tell on them, after one of his friends told me everything that night in bed." She buried her face in her hands and wept. "I thought he was going to kill me!" She sobbed.

He came over and sat with her on the sofa, cradling her damp shoulders in his large embrace. "It's OK. You're safe now," he assured her. "Stay here tonight, I'll take the couch and in the morning I'll find somewhere safe for you to stay while we get them all behind bars. Where did this happen?"

"At the Paradise Hotel, on the corner of Wiltshire and Connecticut." She sobbed.

"What did this Toledo look like? Would you recognise him again?"

"Yes. He was fairly small built with a short black beard and moustache, he has a pasty kind of face and…"

"Wears a lily in his jacket button hole," Rainey finished her sentence with a grim look on his face.

"Do you know him?" she asked, as he went to the fridge for some ice, stopping briefly to pour her a measure of whiskey in one of his cleanest coffee mugs.

"No, we haven't been properly introduced but I intend to fix that!" he said handing her the bag of ice and the scotch. She winced when she put the cold bag on her darkly bruised cheek and took a swig from the cup. The harsh taste made her bare her teeth as she finished taking a drink and she coughed. "Good grief Rainey, what is this? Paint stripper?" she gasped.

"You're very welcome," he said with a smile. He had seen her in some states in the year or so since he had met her. But this was different; he could tell that she had been badly shaken

51

by her ordeal. "I'll fix you something to eat then you should get some rest, OK?"

Later on, when she was settled and resting sound asleep in his bed, Rainey sat on his sofa as the rain misted against his window with a bottle of beer and some of the case files he had brought from his records at the office. He had rang the precinct and told them what had happened and they responded with several police cars that stormed their way to the hotel she had mentioned. He leafed his way through the heavy documents of eyewitness reports and brief investigation of the crime scenes in the report. The case he was reading was about a group of murders that had taken place within a week. It was from the heavy load of paperwork of menial cases that the top dogs thought funny to drop on him. Something was strange about them, a feeling that he was missing something, a piece of the puzzle that deliciously eluded him. The detectives who had looked into it had branded it as 'some sort of domestic matter'. This was mainly due to the fact that only two of the victims had actually been employed, whereas, the remaining three victims had been welfare cases. It had taken place last year, in early July, and they had seemed totally unrelated to each other. All five victims had been killed with different weapons and methods, but as the report actually said, almost desperately. The only connection to the victims was that they lived in the same neighbourhood, around ten blocks at that.

He settled down on his sofa and turned off the small light on the table. He lay there in his white vest staring at the ceiling, the half-light reflected the dark ripples of rain from his window, like black-beaded tears as they traced away on his ceiling to evaporate into darkness. It was Emily's description of the man Toledo that sent his mind racing. 'The man with a snake on his jacket'. Penny had told him that a crew from Washington was coming within the week to supposedly rob the New York Bank. She had said that they would have to keep the Viper happy, while they were on his territory. The Viper's gang here in New York were a small time gang of petty thugs turned pretty boys. The gang members had been inside prison any number of times but hadn't done anything like murder before. Rainey decided to pay the gang's leader a visit tomorrow to see if he could shake something loose on the killing of the man from number five, in Emily's back alley. He only knew the gang leaders name from the reports he had read at the station.

Johnny (Snakebite) Jones.

The next morning he woke up with the sun in his eyes, he squinted and blinked at the window, where hardly any of the raindrops had survived the sunlight. He smacked his dry lips and heaved himself off the sofa. He looked with bleary eyes into the bedroom but saw that Penny had long since gone, just the pulled back blankets from the bed and a note on the pillow. He went to the coffee pot and started to boil some water. He yawned and stretched as he went to pick up the note, it read, 'Thank you for looking after me. Sorry I had to run, but I had to get back and feel normal. A scared hooker doesn't pay the rent. I'll be OK and in contact soon. Have a cup of paint stripper ready for me! Love Penny'. He smiled as he went to finish making his hot coffee, then noticed something in the bed sheets. It was the glint of gold coloured metal, attached to a turquoise pearl like earring, that caught his attention. It was cheap and tacky, a dime a dozen in the local flea market, all to make her more attractive to her undiscerning customers. He smiled to himself as he picked it up.

It was a juddering, staggered rush he felt, a thickness in his head that made him feel nauseous and sick in the pit of his gut. When the blackness cleared, like waking from passing out, he was looking through Penny's eyes straight at Toledo. His small face and immaculately thin beard, pale skin and dark eyes bored into hers as he spoke to her. He was wearing his black coat and waistcoat and Rainey could clearly see the white lily in his coat button hole.

"You know what to do!" he said. His voice was well-spoken, almost like a man of the theatre, very eloquent and at the same time deep and imposing.

"Yes," she said timidly.

"It's going to be alright. There's no turning back. The writings on the wall. Johnny had his turn and now it's yours.

Do it for love, do it for your sister. Always remember that you are my queen. It's take or be taken in this world, so be at the docks by midnight. This part of New York depends on you. If nothing else, think of your reward and a life that before, you could only dream of."

He dropped the earring back on the bed and doubled over, a thick sweat on his brow. He was breathing erratically as he lay on the mattress staring at the earring as weak and sick as a new born child. "Oh my God, not Penny!" he gasped.

He lay there for the longest time. How long he couldn't have said. His mind was replaying the vision from the earring over and over; no sooner that it had finished it began again, like the tender words of a lover said for the final time. Eventually, he felt a little better and his arms and legs regained their strength. Slowly and almost painfully, he hauled himself off of the bed with only one thought echoing in his mind.

He had to save Penny.

He turned the heat off under the water and quickly got dressed, snatched his coat from the wooden stand by the door, swiping his car keys as he pulled his coat on. He flew down the iron-wrought staircase to burst through the wooden doors to the entrance of his block and startled Stretch.

"Hey, Rainmaker. You scared the black outta me!" he said, disgruntled.

"Did you see Penny leave?" he harshly asked him.

"Easy, Rainmaker! Sure I saw her leave, she got picked up in one of them fancy black limos. A man got out and said she was expected. I'm guessing her customers are a bit more flash these days," Stretch told him.

"Thanks, Stretch! Say hi to your mom for me, OK?" Rainey replied, already at the sidewalk running for his car.

He drove fast, weaving in and out of the downtown traffic as he passed a multitude of angry horns and abusive language. He made his way to the Viper's hideout in Lower West Side that ran along the banks of the Hudson river. It was a condemned building of concrete and was scheduled for demolition, years ago. It backed onto the wide chill of the river and the wind whistled through the street as he pulled up outside the wire gates, the name Snakepit was written in black paint on the outside wall. He slipped up beside it as the car's engine throbbed and echoed against it in the golden sunshine. He sat there for a moment, looking down the narrow backstreet to the water at the far end, the sun's rays glittering on the swell of the surface. He wasn't in the mood for conversation and not in the mood for pleasantries, he needed answers and he needed them now. If Johnny knew something, like his vision had told him, then one way or another he was going to talk. He knew he only had until midnight and he knew Penny was in danger. His vision had not revealed where on the docks she had to go and Toledo had told her and that Johnny had already had his turn. Johnny was going to be his only hope of discovering who this sinister man with the lily was, and though he hated to admit it, he was going to need the help of the other so-called detectives.

He shut the engine off and stepped out of the car, adjusting his gun holster for a little more comfort, he had considered taking the shotgun but he didn't want to risk Johnny running in the event that he might have to use it. He marched boldly up to the gate where two men inside the ruined courtyard stood talking and smoking, with baseball bats in their hands. They were wearing the signature brown leather jackets with the picture of a snake on the back. Both of the young men turned when Rainey slapped the metal wire gate with his hand, making it shiver and rattle.

"Beat it old man!" one of the men said with an amused smile.

"I need to see Johnny," Rainey told him.

"Yeah, sure old man! You'll be seeing Saint Peter if you don't get lost!" he sneered.

Rainey shrugged. "OK, you can tell him that you sent Toledo's message away. I'm sure he will understand. See you around boys, unless, of course, you see Saint Peter first!" he said indifferently and then started to walk back to his car. The metal gate opened quickly as the two men almost ran out after him.

"Hey, now! Sorry about that, sir, we get a lot of cranks calling y'know! Here let us escort you to Johnny, it will be our pleasure," one of them said smiling, as they walked him inside.

Rainey looked about as the two men made idle, pleasant chit-chat with him to try and ease the situation. The big detective noticed that they were the only ones in the courtyard and he could only see another two standing by one of the fallen out walls at the front on the top floor. They all went through the large sliding metal doors at the entrance; it made an eerie hollow grating sound as the talkative guard pulled it open. He waited until the other man turned to close it and pretended to reach for his cigarettes inside his coat. He then whipped his closed fist in a quick arch and struck the chatty guard on the side of the temple; he recoiled with the blow then slumped over with his eyes rolled back. Then, without flinching, he swung the same closed fist in an arch the opposite way to strike the other man on the back of the neck, knocking him out cold as well. "Take a break boys." He grimaced and then started to make his way up to the top floor. As he moved up onto the second floor, he saw that some walls had been knocked out here to make a large lounge area, there were tattered sofas, tables littered with empty beer cans and even a scattering of beds. This was obviously the Viper's common room where they relaxed at the end of the day. As he made it to the top floor, the two men that had been standing by the fallen out wall came to meet him at the top, crowbars at the ready. Rainey smiled as he approached and then whipped his gun from its holster to level at the men, a finger held up over his smiling mouth. He motioned them over to an iron bar that was standing rigid from the concrete floor, probably an old support column at one point. The two men put their weapons on the floor and then sat by the bar side by side at the big man's motion with his gun. Rainey then cuffed them together and then holstered his colt.

"Is he alone?" Rainey whispered, showing the two men his detective's shield.

"No, he's got his girl with him. He don't like to be disturbed when she calls," one of the men said with a nasty sneer on his face.

Rainey stooped and patted his face quite hard. "Thanks. You want to be careful pulling a face like that! If the wind changes it will stay that way!" he told him with a smirk.

He then walked toward the double doors that lead to the Snakebite's throne room and pushed them open. They swung open with force as he walked in and saw Johnny sat on a large makeshift concrete throne. It had been constructed with the large blocks that had come from the demolition of the building and was padded out with large red cushions. A scantily clad girl was lying across his lap and he was whispering to her with a seductive smile. The rest of the large room was adorned with hanging drapes from the wall, probably stolen from an old theatre, along with an actual chandelier with many candles in place of the normal electric bulb fittings. Johnny didn't look up as he nibbled on the giggling girl's ear, as Rainey came striding along his dirty maroon carpet.

"I told you, I'm busy boys," he said absently without taking his eyes off of the young girl.

"Yeah, sorry about that Johnny. I must have missed that message," Rainey told him in his deep voice.

Johnny looked at him sharply and so did the startled girl. "How the hell did you get in here?" he demanded then shouted past the big man stood in front of him in his long grey coat and black hat. "Fang! Rattle!"

"Oh, they said they could not make it, your Highness. They're a little tied up at the moment," Rainey told him, sombrely. His eyes then moved to the girl who looked a little terrified. "Beat it, honey. I've got some business with his Majesty here." She didn't need asking twice and swung off his lap, gathered the rest of her clothes in her arms and hurried past Rainey as he stood staring at Johnny who sat uncomfortably on this concrete throne. He started to comb his black, slick hair that was fashioned a lot like an Elvis-type style, trying to look a little more composed after being caught off guard.

"What do you want?" he demanded brashly as he went to put his comb away. Rainey was about to answer him when Johnny hastily yanked out a snub-nose .38 revolver from beneath one of his large cushions.

It was smooth and quicker than the eye could blink, the practiced action of an experienced gunfighter. A motion spent months of years perfecting, Rainey's hand was a blur as he swept his .45 from its holster, aimed and blasted out a single shot. It echoed inside the large room with a flash of fire and a cloud of gun smoke, the bullet caught the side of the .38 and sent it flying out of Johnny's hand to land with a bump on the carpet far behind him. Johnny sat forward holding his jarred hand in pain, as Rainey stood with a grim face with his colt levelled at the startled man, gun smoke still drifting from the muzzle of the black automatic. Rainey glared at him angrily through the grey smoke.

"A little cooperation would be nice," he growled with his teeth bared.

He walked slowly toward him, briefly showing him his detective's badge with the gun still levelled at him. "I know, you know the man they call Toledo. I also know that you murdered a man in the alley of Washington and Maine the other night. What I don't know is why and where it's going to happen next. You are going to help enlighten me, Mr Snakebite, one way or another!" Rainey told him, raising his voice slightly so that he had Johnny's attention.

"I, I don't know what you're talking about, man! It wasn't me! I don't know anything about what you're talking about!" the injured Johnny stammered.

Rainey didn't hesitate and his face grew darker as he was still walking forward, slowly starting to lose his temper and his patience, he fired another shot. The ringing blast once again echoed around the room as the bullet blew away the corner of the concrete throne next to Johnny's head, exploding it in a grey powder. Johnny cried out in terror.

"I really hate repeating myself! Where is TOLEDO?" Rainey started to yell.

All Johnny could see was the muzzle of the .45, as Rainey once again pointed it towards Johnny's head. "I can't tell you, man! You don't know what you're dealing with, he's capable of anything! It was a fair move! I can't tell you! My families' lives depend on it! You're just going to have to lock me up or kill me!" Johnny shouted back with tears in his eyes. Rainey had walked straight up to Johnny now and had placed the muzzle on his forehead. Rainey slowly pulled the hammer back on his colt, his eyes were alight with anger, as they bore into Johnny's terrified green ones.

"I mean it!" he growled deeply.

"Please! I can't, you don't understand! Please!" Johnny whimpered, closing his eyes as he waited for the big man to pull the trigger.

Rainey stood over him for a moment, a fiery rush coursing through his body and mind as his temper was drowning out reason. He was breathing hard, half tempted to just pull the trigger and yet the voices of reason and temperance echoed back at him, Of how the many fights he had with his wife had always been created by his loss of temper and his moody behaviour. He didn't realise it then but his lack of control on his emotions had effectively destroyed everything he had loved. He blinked then a couple of times, like he was waking from a bad dream as he realised what he was doing and pulled the gun away from the sobbing man's forehead. It was obvious that he wasn't going to talk, that the repercussions of him saying anything would be far greater than anything Rainey or the police department could do to him.

"Give me your hand!" Rainey ordered him. Johnny's tear-streaked face looked at him with a questioning look.

"What?" he sniffed, pulling his hands closer to his stomach defensively. Rainey lowered his gun toward his groin and looked at him seriously.

"Give me your hand, or I'm sure your girl will find another fella," he told him with a wave of the colt suggestively toward the middle of his legs. Reluctantly and extremely unsure, Johnny held out his uninjured hand toward the big man still shaking with shock.

"Don't move!" Rainey told him and then reached out and took his hand in his own large one.

It was a slow gurgling rush this time, as though the normal feeling of the wall of sand had been soaked in water. He could feel the warmth and pulse of Johnny's heart and his echoed thoughts in the vaults of his mind; they were incoherent as if they were all speaking at once behind a wall of wool. He was clearly aware that it was very different this time as he was not connected through an inanimate object, but with a living breathing human being. It began as a staccato of flashing images at first, brief flash bulb moments within Johnny's life. He was running with his brothers in the streets of Chicago, his old leather shoes slapping on the wet cobbled street as they laughed together in grey cloth caps, long shorts with grubby faces and skinned knees, knocking on people's doors and then running away. It flashed forward, then in a rush of still like images, they went quick, like flicking through an animation of picture cards. Rainey found that if he tensed his mind he could slow them into focus. They slowed and stopped with the face of a cute blonde girl and the first time he had ever kissed, then moved to the first time he had fallen in love. They were images of lost summer days walking through wheat fields together, talking idly. Then it slipped forward again to the face of another man who he was arguing with, as the blonde girl stood behind that man and laughed at Johnny. Rainey felt bitterness and jealousy as Johnny's heartbreak. He then saw Johnny's trip to New York with his small, brown case on his lap as he sat looking out quietly at the Harbour while the Statue of Liberty slipped slowly past. The images went fast then, a blur of fragments and feelings as they swept through Rainey's mind. A mass of teasing images fractured by, as he felt sorrow, pain and then darkness. The images changed with the flashing of other men's faces, all smiling and talking to him, he suddenly felt the anger in Johnny become blanketed with a feeling of belongingness, as a group of likeminded individuals came together. Then he felt nothing but greed and the darkness that fuelled it. The images finally slowed after a time to the point where Rainey had ordered him to give him his hand, and he could feel fear in Johnny's heart and uncertainty. Rainey concentrated then, trying to stop all of Johnny's thoughts and memories swarm over his current one. It was difficult like trying to keep the tide from the shore, as the big man slowly let the memories slide back from that moment. He saw everything that had happened before, he saw Johnny's girl walk in and slowly undress in front of him, and then when he had got up that morning, although the images were going backward, they were still somehow playing forward. It was a bizarre and unexplainable feeling. He then saw Johnny at the stall at Joe's as he read the letters and numbers on the wall and wrote them down on the back of his hand, before wiping them into a smear. The next scene in his mind was Johnny sitting in the passenger seat of a car riding toward their rundown hideout. He had turned in his seat to talk to his gang members.

"It's on for tonight at Washington and Maine 57th street, apartment 5. We are gonna be rich boys!" he told them laughing.

The talking in the car became just a bustle of excitement and some of concern as Johnny coolly waved it off as he reassured them that it was all going to be OK. The sound was swallowed until it became an echoing reverberation, as Rainey went further back.

He was finally looking through Johnny's eyes not far from Emily's back alleyway, waiting in the rain, feeling nervous and at the same time excited and scared. He watched from a dark recess in an apartment wall as a shiny black Cadillac hummed around the corner, slipping through the sheet of hissing rain. This was the night that David Ellis had died, or as Emily had put it, "The nice man from number 5." Rainey relaxed a little allowing himself to merge with the memory as the driver climbed out and opened a black umbrella as he walked around briskly to open the back door for his passenger. The man with the lily and the smart short black coat had climbed out, taking the umbrella from his driver. His face, however, was still smudged, like someone had left a thumbprint on the glass of the camera Rainey was watching him through. He was irritated by this and wondered why the vision wouldn't show him the face of the man called Toledo.

"This is indeed a momentous night for me and you, Mr Jones, and one that the House of Cards will not forget." Toledo told him with a spirited tone in his deep theatrical voice. "Everything is set for the next move and it is very important to both you and the House. We will not forget your loyalty for this position, Mr Jones."

"Yes, Mr Toledo. Thank you, sir," Johnny said nervously.

The small man placed his black gloved hands gravely on Johnny's shoulders and regarded him seriously. "You do remember the rules don't you, Mr Jones? No one runs and no one talks! I have your money with me and your family in Chicago are having a wonderful time at a very nice club called the Ritz. They are being entertained by some very good friends of mine, so let's not spoil their evening," he said, sombrely leaving the answer hanging in the air.

Johnny nodded quickly with an understanding face.

"Jolly good!" Toledo said, again with that upbeat tone in his voice. He then handed Johnny a stiletto dagger, thin and pointed and then motioned toward the alleyway. "Shall we?" he asked pleasantly.

They both stood at one end of the drenched alley, the rain pattering fast on the small man's umbrella as they looked at a similar gathering at the other end. A man dressed in a blue denim jacket and jeans was standing next to the lady in purple under an umbrella, she was whispering to him as Johnny and Toledo stood watching. She handed the man a different weapon to Johnny's, a very sharp sword, it was slender and quite long, and the blade caught the light from the street lamps outside, as he turned it over in his hands.

"I have total confidence in you, sir!" Toledo assured him. Then the lady looked toward the sinister little man and nodded and he nodded back. "It's take or be taken my boy, do the House proud!" He then patted him on the back and shrunk out of the way, as did the purple lady, leaving the two men to face each other in the rain.

David Ellis was the man in denim and he had obviously never held a sword before. He walked stiffly as the two men neared each other, a look of desperate panic on his face. Johnny's mind was on his family and the large sum of money in Toledo's car. It was David that swung first, holding the hilt of the weapon with two hands in a ferocious swipe at Johnny's head. The man in the snake jacket swept under it skilfully as his opponent swung it back the same way, his teeth gritted in panic. The blade sang through the air, cutting through the raindrops into a small spray, as once again Johnny weaved out of the way. He then retaliated in a series of small sweeping slashes toward David who stumbled back awkwardly. He had forced him back toward the rear of the alley, gripping the sword handle until his knuckles went white, then in a clumsy yet powerful move swept the sword over his head to bring it down on Johnny. As he raised it, Snakebite lunged forward driving his dagger cleanly into the panicked man's heart, killing him instantly. He fell backward in a slump and landed in a crumpled sprawl, exactly where Rainey had found him that night.

"Congratulations, sir! Well taken! It was a fair move. You've done well, Mr Jones! Come, I'll give you a ride home. I have champagne on ice in the car," Toledo complemented him.

"Thank you, Mr Toledo," Johnny replied, still out of breath.

Rainey felt exhausted and also felt himself let go of Johnny's hand. A slip through wet sand later, he was looking at the nervous man, who sat on his concrete throne.

"What was all that about? Why did you hold my hand then let go?" he asked Rainey, not sure exactly what had happened. Rainey had felt he had been in his vision for hours, but in reality it was only a mere matter of seconds. Rainey's brow was sweating and he was breathing a little hard.

"Jonathan Jones, you are under arrest for the murder of David Ellis, if you have anything to say, wait until I have my breath back!" Rainey told him.

Act Five
Marching Towards Midnight

It was mid-morning by the time the police officers had made their arrests at the hideout near the Hudson and gone through the paperwork to lock them up. They also had the word out on the police band to be on the lookout for the rest of the gang. Johnny was screaming and shouting, as they struggled to put him in the back of one of the squad cars. He was yelling about how Rainey was a madman, that Rainey was going to kill him. He was also crying out about police brutality and that Rainey had touched him, that he was weird and had done something to Johnny. Even though, the police officers ignored for the most part what Johnny was saying, Rainey did catch them looking at him a little strangely.

It was Sam Peters who was at the station booking them in, and had been given the task of going through the mountain of paperwork that went with it. Rainey recognised him from the crime scene the other night; he was a lean solidly built man with a very strong jaw line. He was dependable, well-liked and respected amongst the community and his fellow officers. He was the kind of person who didn't let anything get him down, professional and polite, even in the face of intolerable abuse. That kind of thing was a day to day thing for Sam and he seemed to take it all in his stride. Rainey liked him, he was the kind of man who was good to have on your back in a fight and he also had a really nice car. It was the subject of envy amongst his fellow officers as they stood admiring it on brief coffee breaks through the windows of the station. It was a gold and chrome Pontiac GTO, a real statement of an American muscle car. It was always kept clean and shiny, showing its bold lines and drilled holed chrome mags within its sport tyres, the twin head lights made up the front of an intimidating machine, indeed. Sam was a single man, he had no wife or children and no girlfriend as far as anyone knew, so his money was pretty much his own. He spent a lot of time on active duty and seemed to let himself become absorbed with work, foregoing any kind of social life. It was no secret within the police community that Sam wanted, one day, to become a detective and had put his first request in just barely a week beforehand.

"Hey Sam, nice work rounding them all up," Rainey told him as he stood in front of the man's desk.

"Thanks, Detective. What led you to find the killer so quickly?" Sam asked.

"Let's just say it took a lot of looking into," Rainey smiled.

"That reminds me; Sharpe is upstairs and keeps asking if you're back yet, he didn't sound happy," Sam told him.

"I didn't know you had time to go upstairs, Sam!"

"I didn't, we can all hear him down here!" Sam said with raised eyebrows. Rainey laughed as he walked upstairs giving Sam a quick salute of thanks, readying himself for his inevitable grilling.

As he walked into the detective's office floor to the usual bustle, his mind was racing. There were still so many things that were unanswered and he was trying to make some sense out of it. He sat at his desk, where a fresh bunch of paperwork was waiting for him; he scrolled a sheet of paper into his typewriter and began to make his report on the events of the morning's arrests. As he typed, he noticed that the top report on his tray was from the officer that had been called to the Paradise Hotel, the place Penny had told him the out-of-town gang was staying at, where she had received the slap on her face. He stopped typing and picked it up, the officer who had filed the report said that there was no one matching the description of the men from Washington ever checking into the Hotel. Rainey frowned in surprise. It wasn't like Penny to be wrong, normally her information was spot on and had led to many arrests in the past. Then again these last couple of days had been anything but normal. He wanted to dismiss the idea that she might have lied about it, the men might have decided to lay low for a bit and paid the owner of the Hotel off, so that they wouldn't talk. Failing that, they may have abandoned their scheme altogether, and settled for a more vulnerable target. Rainey marked it as a report, not to be dismissed, and that for now it would remain priority. He knew it would get shelved, the truth was there simply wasn't the time or manpower to go and follow it up, it was a case of waiting for something to happen and then following that up. In this city and at this time, they had neither prevention nor cure, it's just the way it was, and all anyone could do was their best for the city and hope that it would somehow be enough. His train of thought had led him back to what Johnny had said, when he had confronted him at the hideout. It hadn't made sense to him and his loss of temper had made his head numb to what he was saying, "It was a fair move," he had said. Could it mean that the confrontation in the alley was some sort of bizarre initiation into this mysterious organisation known as the House of Cards? Could it also be linked to the five murders that had taken place in the same vicinity in early July? He then wondered if Penny had been seduced into the same thing that Johnny had been. The vision that he had got from her earring had shown him Toledo telling her that, "*Johnny has had his turn and now it was hers.*" He had also told her, "*Do it for your sister.*" If Toledo was willing to pay that kind of money for a one-on-one with another nobody, maybe to gain entrance for a position in the House, she may well have been tempted. He didn't know much about Penny, apart from what she did and who she did it for, maybe she had a sister somewhere who needed an operation. Maybe her sister had gotten herself into debt with a loan shark. Whatever the reason, he knew that whatever the amount of money was being paid, murder was still murder and he didn't want to see his friend go down that road.

However, he could take consolation from the one thing he did know. The vision that he had got from Johnny had revealed the way to solve the puzzling letters and numbers that had been written in Joe's restroom. WM meant Washington and Maine, 57 had meant 57th street and the last number 05 had been the apartment number of the next contestant. It was all very cryptically clever.

Toledo had said it himself to Penny. "*The writing's on the wall.*" It was just a hunch that maybe he was referring to that but it did make sense and it was a step in the right direction. His thoughts were shattered by Sharpe's voice yelling from his office door.

"Rainey! Get in here NOW!" he bellowed.

He stood from his desk and looked across at the usual gathering of the four other detectives, who sat around Newman's desk. Newman was the fresh-faced son of the Commissioner and the other three were his so-called friends, basking in his status. Randall, Barnes and Fredrick were all detectives only because Newman had not wanted to go at it alone, and also to please his father by doing something worthwhile with his life. They all smiled knowingly at him, as he took his long coat off and hung it on the back of his chair, his white shirt and holstered gun snugly clung snugly to his large torso. They were all whispering as he neared them and chuckling below their breath. He stopped briefly by Newman's desk with a broad smile on his face.

"You know it makes me feel all warm and fuzzy to see a group of perfectly matched couples, you should really think about getting engaged," he said sincerely.

"For your information Jasper, we have all been assigned a very important task," Newman replied stiffly.

Rainey smiled. "Oh wait, let me guess, make-up tips?"

"You'll be laughing on the other side of your face when Sharpe gets through with you, gypsy man!" retorted Barnes. He was slightly more portly than the others, who obviously spent a lot of time looking in their mirrors in the morning.

"Very good, Barnes! That was almost an insult! Not very original but still a very good effort. Call me that again and the other side of your face will look really stupid without any teeth!" Rainey said mockingly. Barnes seemed to shrink back a bit at that comment.

"I've got to go now, girls. You have fun with your lipstick colours," Rainey said, still smiling as he walked toward the office, where Sharpe sat behind his desk looking extremely irritated. Rainey walked in and closed the door as Newman and his friends all turned to watch him through the office window.

"What in hell's name do you think you're doing Rainey?" he yelled at him.

"I believe the term is detective. I'm detecting things, and some of your boys should try it some time," Rainey replied mildly.

"Your job is exactly what job I give you! You are supposed to be behind your desk looking into missing persons and going through unsolved minor cases that have been backing up for two years!" Sharpe told him, still yelling.

"Yes Chief, that's usually the definition of the word detective."

"That's really funny, Rainey. I must remember that one for the policeman's ball! You aren't anywhere near as smart as you are funny! What the hell are you doing arresting the Jones boy?"

"He murdered a man in cold blood the other night; I thought that might be relevant," Rainey replied, still in a calm tone.

"What's relevant to me is the statement I just got from downstairs!"

"I'm assuming that that's a polite word for interrogation?"

"If you know what's good for you Rainey, do not interrupt me again!" Sharpe growled. "His statement tells me that you shot at him with intent to kill! And when he protested his innocence, you wanted to touch him! I don't know what you were trying to do there! Maybe some sort of Gypsy curse! I want to believe that this was all nonsense, the department doesn't need this kind of publicity and I don't need any loose cannons! Am I making myself clear?" he barked but then carried on without waiting for a reply. "Two of his gang members who were interviewed, separately, said that they distinctly heard gunfire, this was, of course, after you had assaulted two of them and then handcuffed another two without probable cause! I'm assuming that you have some extremely solid evidence to support your arrest?"

Rainey knew he was going to struggle here, knowing wasn't enough, he had to somehow prove it. He already knew what the Chief thought of him, so telling him he had a vision about it would be about enough to see him laughed off the force for good.

"I went there on a tip off from a very reliable source that put him at the murder scene and at the time of Mr Ellis's death; I was merely trying to scare him when he refused to talk," Rainey lied smoothly.

"Well things don't work like that around here, Rainey!"

"It's not the only thing that doesn't work around here," Rainey replied, looking out the window to where Newman and his friends were sneering and chuckling amongst themselves, he knew his comment would change the subject and if nothing else buy a bit more time to get something concrete on Johnny.

Sharpe stood up quickly, biting on the end of his cigar and pushing his chair back with a scrape. "Now you listen to me! I've had about enough of your mouth, Detective! Those men happen to be in charge of a major investigation into a threat from a large organisation. I don't want you trampling all over it with your off the handle theories and methods. I don't want you anywhere near the case they're working on, and that includes the Jones boy!"

"Let me guess the House of Cards?" he replied almost absently.

Sharpe looked at him with a piercing stare, almost biting the end of his cigar off. "I don't know how you know that, but I'm going to pretend that I didn't hear it! I don't want you in any way interfering with this. I want you back at your desk and I want you going through the files of all the hookers, the junkies and the rest of the gypsy scum in New York! Because that's where you belong! You leave the real work to us and you will get to play detective a little while longer. Now get out of my sight!"

Rainey looked at him with a face like thunder and then turned and opened the door. "I can't imagine why the FBI turned you down," he said loudly, so everyone could hear him. "Because you have the makings of a man who could get a diploma in BS!" He then closed the door and made his way back to his desk. The four detectives all went back to their desks with their heads down as if they were working, waiting for the silence in the room to clear.

The door reopened and Sharpe came out with a face the colour of beetroot. "Newman get in here! I hope those reports are up to date!" he bellowed.

Newman almost tipped his chair over as he rushed to stand up; his eyes were just like a rabbit caught in a car's headlights.

Rainey knew what that was about, if Sharpe knew the existence of this House of Cards and the fact that he had inadvertently defended Johnny from it, meant that he knew more about what was going on than anyone else. Rainey knew that there was more to this than what he himself had uncovered. But that wasn't priority right now, it was finding Penny before she could make a terrible mistake, and that meant finding Toledo, time was running out.

He sat pondering over the problem at his desk and reached for his coffee cup for a drink but it was empty, he stood and went over to the coffee percolator as he thought about how he was going to find Toledo. He knew he had told Penny to be at the docks but didn't say where, he did say midnight so at least Rainey did know when. If Penny was going to go at this bizarre initiation, then he would need to know where to go to face the initiation. His thoughts then flashed back to the vision that he had at Joe's and the woman in the purple dress, she had slipped Toledo that code on a napkin and Johnny's vision had told him how to read them. "Sometimes I can be so dumb!" he muttered to himself, his eyes lighting up with realisation. He quickly went back to his desk and put his coffee down, then went through his coat pocket to get his notebook. After flicking the pages over and going through the notes he had made in the last few days, he found what he was looking for. It was circled in pencil at the bottom of the page, WM5621. It was the code that had been written under the first one, which meant he knew where Penny would be tonight, and more importantly where Toledo would be. He smiled to himself knowing that this time he had the upper hand. Toledo didn't know he was coming and that the element of surprise was going to be his best weapon here; he didn't want to waste it.

He then had another thought and looked at the names of the five victims of the area in early July. He stood from his desk and walked over to Sandra, who was filing some documents. She looked up and smiled as he came over.

"Hey Sandra, do you happen to have any maps of the city? Or maybe districts of the city?" he asked her.

"Yeah sure, they're in the records department. Here I'll show you," she said, rising from her chair. She took him out of the room, down a corridor on the right to where people were walking, some running back and forth, most with folders in their hands. The air was alive with mumbled conversations and the ever-present noise of ringing telephones. She took him through a pine looking door and into a quieter room that was lined with shelves of books, graphs and large rolled up maps.

"Here you go, Detective," she said.

"Thanks, Sandra," he replied.

"I hope you find what you're looking for," she said as she left the room.

"I hope so too!" he mumbled to himself and then started looking through the many maps catalogued in the shelving units. After searching through quite a few of them, he finally found one that suited his purpose. It was a district map of downtown NYC, and it was referenced with a grid of each section of streets and the blocks that they ran through. He unrolled the map on one the large tables in the room and used his coffee mug to hold the end down. He then drew out his colt .45 and laid it on the other edge to stop it rolling up. He stood looking at the map and absorbed it, his eyes flickering

71

over the various grids, his pencil tapping thoughtfully on his chin. After a moment, he opened his notebook and started to look down the list of the victims and the locations in which they had been murdered; he also took a note of the dates.

"OK Jasper, what exactly are you looking for?" he asked himself in a whisper.

He started to list the people that had been killed in July, he marked the position on the map where they had died and the area relevant to that person's address.

"OK the first victim was Norah Davis and she was murdered here," he said marking a cross on the map. "And this is where she lived," he said also marking it on the map. "Next we have Giovanni Silverado…"

He spent a while going through them, and also marked some of the unsolved murders of the homeless and supposedly missing persons from previous years on the map. In fact, he had marked any homicide on the map that had another one close to it and had a similar sort of pattern. By the time he had finished, it was early afternoon and he had just marked the last victim that Johnny had killed, David Ellis, on the map. He stopped and rubbed his eyes through the fatigue of looking at the same document for hours and then stood back to view what he had done. The first thing that struck him was the position of the murders in association with the addresses of the victims, it all seemed rather symmetrical, occasionally staggered in parts but other than that, rather neat even in a haphazard way. He frowned in confusion as he stared at it trying to make sense of it, he had traced back quite a few murder cases over the last few years and they all seemed grouped here, where poverty seemed to thrive. He then thought back to the woman and Toledo in the bar and the code they used to determine, where and who would be competing next for a place within the House. Almost like some sort of premeditated move. His eyes dawned then with a terrible realisation and looked at the map again. He remembered what Toledo had said to Johnny, "*It was a fair move.*" Even Johnny himself had shouted it at him when Rainey had pushed for answers. Toledo had told Penny that she was his queen,

Toledo had also told Johnny that his move was most important and that the House of Cards would not forget his loyalty to their position. "It's take or be taken," Rainey murmured to himself, repeating Toledo's words.

"Oh my God!" Rainey said with a dreadful horror, chilling his blood. "It's a game of chess! They're using people of poverty as chess pieces!"

He looked back feverishly at the map and counted the grids that contained the groups of killings over the years and came up with the number 64, just like the diameter of a chess board. David Ellis had been given a sword to fight with, just like a knight. Johnny had been given a dagger, probably the weapon of a priest or in this case, a bishop.

He marked the position of Johnny's kill and then followed it up to where he lived at the hideout, it was a perfect diagonal. David Ellis had lived at apartment 5 in the neighbourhood where he had died and Rainey traced it back to where he was killed. It was L-shaped, three blocks up and one block over. Rainey figured out that the woman in purple must be Toledo's opponent and that instead of risking an all-out mob war which would attract attention, they use the poor and homeless to play their game, where the death of such people would cause less of an impact on the city. Rainey thought that the winner gained control of the board and therefore, seizes territory. The same person was not used twice, so as to keep them from the hands of the law and thus, not risking exposure. A new piece would be selected from the capture square, taking over the last piece's move.

Rainey wasn't the best chess player but he knew enough of the pieces had been taken to know that the game would soon be over, that's why Toledo needed her—she was his queen. He grabbed the map up and ran from the records room to see Sharpe with his discovery. He knew he wasn't going to help, but at least he would know that Rainey was doing it by the book. When he got to the office, Sharpe and the other four detectives had left, he dumped the map on his desk to show Sharpe later and grabbed his coat. If he was quick enough he could make it to the place where the next move was going to take place, Washington and Maine 56th street apartment 21, to see if he could stop this in its tracks and bring these so-called players to justice. On his way out of the precinct he saw Sam, still at his desk amongst a throng of people sweeping through the station. If he was going to do this, he just might a need a little back up. Sharpe and his so-called detectives were not going to help, so he would have to do this another way. He looked at Sam as he worked through the mass of paperwork on his desk, Sam wasn't like the guys upstairs and would make an ideal man for the help he needed; he decided to pull rank but in a polite way.

He had a sincere look on his face as he approached Sam's desk. "Hey Sam, listen I need you to leave early, I need your help."

Sam gave him a look from above the file he was holding. "I have a ton of paperwork here, Detective. Can't someone from your department help?"

"I'm afraid it's not as simple as that, I need to follow up a lead and Sharpe is busy with some sort of task force," Rainey told him gravely. Sam lowered his file onto his desk and regarded Rainey with his brown eyes.

"What you really mean to say is, no one upstairs will go anywhere near you because Sharpe doesn't want you interfering with his case. That's why he assigned you to missing persons and a list of unsolved cases as long as your arm. So you need someone from the body of non-detective personnel to help you without him knowing, right?" Sam told him.

"Yeah that's pretty much it, Sam. Except one tiny little detail," Rainey replied humbly.

"Really what's that then?"

Rainey looked around at the mass of officers that were running around and answering telephones during the course of the rush of their day. "I came to you out of all the other able people here; I thought you were a man that was doing the decent thing for the city and the department, a man that would excel at doing a little undercover detective work, even if it meant that it was off the record. A friend of mine is in very real danger and I need someone I can rely on to help me out," Rainey told him with a sigh. "I was just hoping it would be you Sam. I guess I was wrong."

He then went to move from the desk with a faintly disappointed look on his broad face, when Sam caught his arm.

"Now, just a minute!" he said tersely under his breath as he caught the big man's eyes with a narrowed look. "I'm one of the first through that door in the morning and I'm one of the last to leave! I happen to take my duty very seriously! I didn't say that I wouldn't help, I just wanted to know if you were going to be straight with me! If I get caught up in this, I could lose my badge!"

"Not if you are working under my orders you won't, does that mean you'll help?" Rainey asked, as Sam released his arm and sat back down in his chair. He didn't answer for a minute and looked as if he was having a private conversation with himself in his mind.

"Hey, Pete," he said, looking over at a tall black man who was studying a folder at his desk. "Could you file these for me? I've got to run an errand with the detective here."

Pete stood up from his chair; he was tall and strongly built. "Sure thing, Sam," he replied in an unusually deep voice. Sam stood up as Pete walked over and then came around the desk to stop in front of Rainey.

"Thanks, Sam. You'll make a detective yet," Rainey said with a smile.

"I just know I'm going to regret this." Sam said, as they walked toward the doors that led to the locker room. "I didn't know you had friends?"

Rainey ignored that.

After Sam had changed into his black leather jacket and jeans he met Rainey at the side street, a way down the road from the station. The big man watched, as Sam's gold GTO cruised down the street toward him with a heavy throb from the engine with the sun running over the gleaming bodywork. He couldn't help but admire his car and the absolute attention to its clean and pristine condition; Sam was obviously a man who took care of the things he loved. Rainey felt slightly embarrassed that he hadn't washed his black Cadillac in a couple of weeks and hastily stashed some empty cigarette packets and empty food wrappers under the passenger seat as Sam got out of his car to come and sit in his.

"Nice car, Detective," Sam said as he got in and closed the door.

Rainey laughed. "It used to be, Sam!"

"OK, so what is it that you are doing exactly? You mentioned something about a friend being in danger?"

Rainey took a breath and began telling Sam about what he knew about the House of Cards and then told him about Johnny's involvement in it. He explained his theories about the discovery he had made in the records room and how this Toledo character had involved his friend, Penny. In fact, Rainey confided in Sam almost everything that had happened in the last couple of days. He knew how it sounded and even though he was sounded convincing, he knew that the one question Sam was going to ask would blow some serious holes in it all. Sam was in shock by the time Rainey had finished telling him about the next address, Penny being at the docks by midnight, and how he hoped this would give them an upper hand on Toledo.

Time was running out.

"That's quite the story, Rainey! How did you know that Johnny had done the killing in the alley? And how did you know that this man Toledo had told your friend to be at the docks tonight? Where's your evidence, Detective?" Sam asked, amazed at it all.

This was where Rainey knew it could, altogether, fall apart with Sam. He was a level-headed man and only believed in what he could see, sensible and thorough. Rainey had got this far and now he knew he was going to have to take a leap of faith with officer Peters, and hoped that he didn't walk away calling him mad and confirming Sharpe's exaggerated gypsy stories of him.

Rainey looked Sam in the eyes, his face sincere as he drew up the strength to reveal the cause of his investigations. "I need you to keep an open mind here, Sam," he told him gravely.

"OK," Sam replied a little unsurely.

Rainey told him about the incident with his wife's hairbrush, the cigarette and the cigar at Joe's. He told him about Johnny and the earring that had come loose from Penny's ear that night she stayed over. After he had finished telling him he could see Sam was pale and a little shocked, and he half expected him to leave the car in a storm of ignorance.

"I'm not quite sure what to say, Rainey! It's a tall tale by any stretch of the imagination! Let's say I believe you and you really have this gift. Can you use it all the time?"

"It hasn't stopped working yet," Rainey replied with a glimmer of hope that Sam might just believe him.

Sam reached into his jacket pocket and pulled out a pencil, it was half worn down and obviously got used a lot. "OK, I'll tell you what," Sam said. "If you can tell me what I write with this pencil, I'll believe you. It's not something I would tell anyone else, so the only person that knows is me. If you can tell me, I'm with you all the way, if not, you're on your own, OK?"

Rainey nodded, as Sam held the half used pencil toward him and he reached out to take it, feeling a little nervous that of all the times his gift could let him down, this would probably be the moment. Rainey took the pencil from him with his eyes closed and then opened them a moment after to give the pencil back, looking a little blankly at Sam.

"Well, Detective?" Sam asked, also feeling a little nervous. He wasn't exactly sure at this point that it was all some sort of magic trick, he didn't know Rainey that well and the coffee break rumours were starting to creep into his mind.

"Your father is a congressman in Philadelphia. He never approved of you coming here to New York to be a detective and your mother was heartbroken. He told you that if you were ever to keep your inheritance, you must write three letters a week to your mother for comfort. He told you on the steps of his big, white house the morning you left, that if you missed one letter you would be disowned and never allowed back. He said that he would rather comfort your mother for the rest of her life than have you continually disappoint her," Rainey told him.

Sam was obviously choked and his eyes were wet with sadness as he shakily put the pencil back in his pocket. He cleared his throat as he looked out of Rainey's dirty windscreen. "OK, so what's our next move?" he asked with a thick voice.

Rainey thought it was probably best not to dwell on what he had revealed and instead got straight to the point.

"I need a second gun, Sam, in case things don't go to plan; this Toledo character is a very dangerous individual and has gone to a great deal of trouble to hide what he has been doing. I'm just not sure what he his next moved would be. When we get to Washington and Maine, I want you to cover the back door, while I enter from the front. If confronted by Toledo or any other suspect, I want you to shoot to disable, OK? I'm getting you into hot water as it is Sam, I don't need any heroics just a show of force, OK?"

Sam pulled out his .38 revolver from his shoulder holster and looked at it wryly. "I feel I came a little underdressed for the occasion," he said with raised eyebrows.

"Here." Rainey said with a smile as he unlocked the Remington shotgun from his dashboard and passed it to him. "Now you're overdressed! Just remember what I said, OK?"

Sam turned the heavy shotgun over in his hands, as Rainey passed him a box of shells from the glove compartment.

"Careful that thing has quite a kick and things tend to die very easily at the barrel end so only use it if you have to!" he told him with a smile.

Sam nodded confidently. "OK, let's do this!" he said with a set jaw as he pumped the first cartridge into the chamber with a solid, metallic double click.

"You have quite a flair for the dramatic, Sam!" he told him. "Let's get going."

It took them around forty minutes to reach their destination and the roads were already starting to fill with the early evening traffic. The thick veins of white and red lights from the moving traffic filled the crisscross streets of downtown New York, as the darkening sky was a fluid spread of light blue and gold, with the promise of an ever-growing storm cloud in the distance of the skyline. As they neared 56th street, the traffic became quite dense and at one point, Rainey had to get out of his car to show a stubborn truck driver his badge in order to get him to move. As they turned slowly onto the street, the black, dirty Cadillac growled slowly down the front of the street and, the gleaming-gold GTO parted from the road behind him to slip around the back. Sam drove to the top of the entrance of the wide alley-like road and slowed to a stop, the GTO's heavy engine guttered off of the walls as it idled. He observed the littered street and the many rows of stone stairs that lead up to the back doors of the apartments. He could clearly see that halfway down, a black limousine was parked, the lights from the many windows illuminated off its shiny bodywork.

Rainey pulled up to the front and parked a block down from the building with apartment 21. There were some young men outside in the street, to the front steps of the building, who were admiring a friend's new car. It was a yellow Yenko Deuce, a real powerhouse of a car, often used in many races and drag strip events. It was a little worn and was in need of some attention, however, it still had the black tell-tale swoop down its doors leading up to the back end of the car.

Rainey sat behind the wheel and took a breath as he contemplated what to say to the person at the apartment. It was going to be a very awkward conversation. He opened the large door and stepped out into the cooling night air and made his way to the steps of the apartment. He climbed the steps, passing the men who were all talking excitedly to the proud owner of the Deuce. As a precaution he reached under his long coat and unclipped his colt from its holster, he was readying himself for anything while his body slowly filled with adrenaline. The front doors were open and he walked into the main reception area, his shoes echoing from the small green and white tiled, grimy floor as he made his way to the large staircase on his way up to the apartment. He was only five steps up and could hear a muffled conversation from the top as a couple came from around the flight of stairs above him. Rainey only glanced as he made his way up at a rather unconfident woman, who seemed to be walking rather reluctantly. There was a man behind talking reassuringly to her in a low, deep voice.

"It's going to be alright, my dear, you'll see. I have every confidence..." The man's words died in his throat as he saw Rainey look up from the bottom of the stairs to look right back at the man called Toledo.

There was a moment's pause as they both looked unbelievingly at each other, a moment of disbelief frozen in time, just before cold realisation rushed through them both.

Rainey swept his colt from its holster aiming it at the pasty-skinned man. "NYPD, FREEZE!" he yelled.

Toledo stood for a second and gave him a small smile and a nod of acknowledgement, as Rainey held his gun on him, his shoulder in his iron sights.

Act Six
The Cuckoo Howls

Toledo never blinked as he violently pushed the screaming woman down the flight of stairs to land on Rainey, making him lose his aim to catch the hysterical woman. Toledo came halfway down the stairs, as Rainey struggled to get back to his feet with the woman clinging to him in a storm of tears and then vaulted over the banister to land cat like on the tiled floor. He then sprinted toward the back door and to where his limo was parked.

Rainey helped the woman off him and looked at her as he turned to run after him. "Are you, OK? I'll send someone for you try to remain calm, OK?" She just nodded, petrified, as she sat on the steps as her neighbours came out and rushed over to her. Rainey sprinted down toward the back doors to pursue the small man.

Sam had seen the commotion as Toledo had ran from the back doors but had collided with a group of metal trash cans in his desperation to escape; they clattered loudly as the small man stumbled and almost lost his balance. The limo's engine fired into life with a plume of fumes from its twin exhausts, as the driver watched the small man regaining his balance. Sam slammed his car into gear and roared up the alley toward the back of the car, his engine screamed a throaty drum roll that echoed off of the surrounding buildings. He stopped short with a small screech of his back tyres as he whipped out of the car brandishing the Remington shotgun, while Toledo got back to his feet.

"FREEZE!" he yelled at the man.

Toledo pulled a revolver from inside his short well-kept coat and blasted out two shots in succession at Sam, the air clouding with gun smoke. Sam eyes widened with fear as he ducked behind his open car door, one shot shattered his car window covering him with glass and the other struck off the front with a spark and metallic ring as the bullet ricocheted off into the alley. Toledo then ran down the side alley that separated the two apartment blocks as the limo started to drive away in a deep sweeping groan from its engine. Sam stood from his door, his heart banging in his chest as he levelled the shotgun at the escaping car. He blasted the back of the limo, the barrel erupting with a fiery bark as the weapon kicked up with a strong recoil. Sam used the motion to smoothly pump the shotgun again with a double click, sending a spent cartridge flying from the breech in a whisper of smoke, he fired again with a thunderous boom. The back of the fleeing car was peppered with holes as the shotgun decimated the rear, blowing half the bumper off as it hung limply trailing sparks after it. The second blast had completely obliterated the back window shattering glass over the slick ground in the alley. The big car smashed through a pile off stacked boxes and trash as it snaked its way up the alley to join the main road.

It was then Rainey exploded from the back doors and flew down the steps to see the limo sweep off down the alley, he turned to Sam who was pointing with urgency. "The alley! The alley! I've got this one!" he yelled to Rainey. He then got back in his car and peeled off after the limo in a blue haze of smoke, wheel spin and rubber.

Rainey turned and ran down where Sam had pointed just in time to see the well-dressed short man vault with one foot off of the alley's wall to leap from there to the top of a rickety wooden fence gate, which separated the narrow alley between the two blocks. He swept over it very acrobatically to land on the other side running. "Who the hell is this guy?" Rainey said to himself as he ran faster with his teeth gritted toward the gate; his shoulders forward as he braced himself like a battering ram. The sodden, rundown fence gate shattered off its hinges as he collided with a grunt, it splintered outward almost disintegrating as Rainey stumbled out, trying to regain his balance. Toledo had stopped at the mouth of the darkened alley to the entrance of the street beyond; he had turned with his revolver drawn. Rainey used the fact that he was already falling forward to let himself land heavily on the ground behind some metal bins as Toledo shot two echoed blasts from his gun, the bullets whipped past the big man on the floor and Rainey waited a moment before crouching up to return fire. But Toledo was gone only leaving clouding gun smoke to drift in the cool air where he had been standing.

The big man got to his feet with his gun drawn, his coat soiled with the damp ground as he aimed it forward moving quickly and cautiously down the rest of the alley to move out into the darkening early evening hue of street light. He was just in time to see the young group of men looking shocked and afraid by the far end of the apartment steps as their friends Yenko Deuce ripped off down the street. They all pointed as he came out onto the street and started running toward his Eldorado.

"Hey man! He went that way! He stole my car man and he's got a gun!" one young man shouted to Rainey, as he pulled his car door open and started off down the street, his wheels skipping on the tarmac and the thunder of his engine rising in pitch as he began to chase the fast disappearing Deuce. He saw the sinister man swerve left at the top of the street to a mass of angry horns from startled drivers. Rainey was already talking into his police band radio as he thundered up the road after him.

"Rainey to control, I'm in pursuit of a suspect in a stolen yellow Yenko Deuce travelling south on 52nd street. Suspect is armed and extremely dangerous! Also, Officer Sam Peters is in pursuit of a black limo last seen heading north out of 56th street. Assistance required!" he yelled into the handset as he controlled the car with his hand, his knuckles white with tension.

"Roger that, Detective Rainey. Squad cars in the vicinity will be alerted and sent to your assistance. Please be advised that it may take some time before arrival!"

"Perfect!" Rainey growled as he dropped the handset and swerved left onto the street, his tyres squealing as he struggled to keep up with the Deuce. It was a straight rundown the road and the yellow muscle car was gaining speed as it swerved in and out of the traffic, sometimes moving to the wrong side of the road to speed past the slowly moving traffic. There were a couple of cars that had collided with each other resulting in a shattering of lights as Toledo whipped out in front of the oncoming cars, only to swipe back in at the last moment. It was at that moment that Rainey wound the window down, a sweeping breeze of chilling air rushed into the car as he placed his magnetic, red, beacon light on the roof and activated his two-tone wailing siren. The traffic ahead parted either side of the road, allowing him to speed up and close the gap between him and Toledo.

The Eldorado was a lot heavier and the car leaned and swayed on its springs as Rainey followed the Deuce's path up the street. At the next junction, he saw the car turn right, it was going too fast and spun in a torrent of wheel smoke as Toledo hit the brakes hard, after snaking it back into control he shot off again down the road and out of sight. He slowed as he reached the junction and then whipped the black car into the street, it bounced slightly as it turned with a deep screech. Toledo had spun his car completely around when it had disappeared from Rainey's view and he came sweeping back down the street as Rainey pulled onto the road; he even managed a smug salute as he whined past the Cadillac. The big man gritted his teeth and in a screaming swirl of tyre smoke, he spun the heavy car around, smashing his back end into a parked car with a heavy crunch of contacting metal. He then started to tear off after Toledo again, his siren filling the air and his flashing red light reflecting off everything it touched. The top end of the street they were on was blocked by heavy traffic, and Toledo swerved down into a side alley to avoid it; he was heading for the dockyard and the freight train yard. Rainey didn't want to lose him in that mass of freight cars and squeezed the accelerator a little harder; he then swept the car in a controlled screeching skid as he too entered the alley that Toledo had driven down. He could instantly see the smashed trash cans and burst bags of garbage, which now littered the alley floor as the Deuce tore its way through the narrow passage. He followed it down ripping through the wake of destruction that the car had left behind it. The growl of his engine and the smell of the rotting alley filled the inside of his car through the whistling wind whipping in from his open window, the back walls of the apartments blurring either side of him as he tightened his grip on the steering wheel. Toledo went straight across the busy road at the end, narrowly missing the traffic coming from either direction. Rainey held his breath as he came to the end watching the cars blur down the road in front of him, not knowing what was coming on, the want to catch Toledo outweighing judgement and reason as his car bounced out onto the road to the sound of an air horn and the bright headlamps of a truck loaded with iced fish. The truck slammed the side of his buckled car sending it into a swerve as the impact shuddered through the Cadillac. Rainey whipped the wheel this way and that as he struggled to straighten the big car, its tyres complaining loudly as it snaked across the busy road. On the opposite side of the road another car swiped around with a squeal to avoid hitting him as the car behind it smashed into its centre with a shattering of broken headlights and metal. Rainey flew across the road leaving black curved tyre marks on the road as he smashed through metal fence gates that were swinging back shut after Toledo had broken through them.

They were on the black gravel of the freight train yard's ground now and the two cars bounced like kangaroos as they sped along the uneven road towards the risen railway tracks. They bucked high as the two cars leapt over the incline of the tracks and dipped low on impact in a shower of black gravel, sailing briefly through the air to grind again onto the ground and deeper into the train yard. They weaved in and out of the lines of empty freight cars as Toledo desperately tried to lose him in the mass of carriages and engines that sat idly here.

Rainey knew he had him here; the Eldorado was a lot heavier and easier to control on a loose surface, whereas, the Deuce was lighter and had too much torque to gain a substantial grip, making it slip and slide on the gravel. Rainey pulled up at the car's rear side as it slipped slightly in a small shower of black stones. He could hear them sheeting against the car's undersides with a hiss as they blistered through the yard under the legs of the massive cranes that loaded and unloaded the containers from the trains to the ships in the quay beyond. His ears were filled with the garbled sound of the two cars engines and the grating sound of the loose stones as he drew his automatic and aimed at the Deuce. He took aim as the two cars bounced slightly on the uneven surface, running parallel with the Hudson River and the cold sharp wind that swept across its surface. He took a moment to get a good target and then pulled the trigger smartly, the gun's slide snapped back and forth as it jerked slightly, the barrel flash and smoke whipped away by the force of the wind. The first two shots pierced and rang off the car's rear wheel arch, but the third found its mark and the back wheel exploded sending a small wave of gravel from it, as the wheel rim cut into the ground. The car quickly got out of control and slipped into a spin then caught the ground and flipped violently as it barrelled and spun over and over, shattering the windows and crumpling the roof and sides like a beer can. It finally slid onto its buckled roof and impacted into the mounds of gravel piled here and there within the yard. Rainey snapped his attention back to where he was going as he too saw a mound of gravel piled by a crane leg; he hit the brakes hard, but too late as the Cadillac mounted the pile and collided with the huge metal leg, buckling instantly as the radiator burst in a huge cloud of white steam. The car had struck with brutal force, the windscreen had shattered as it had come to a sudden stop with a loud bang of impacted metal; there it sat motionless pointing up at the crane leg, crushed and buckled as the steam from the radiator billowed gently into the cold night air with a constant hiss.

He awoke thick-headed to the sound of two men's voices, his body and bones were seething in hot pain and the cold rain on his head was a small comfort. He groaned as he tried to speak, blood running freely from his mouth as his head thumped the tune of the impact with the steering wheel. It had probably been the impact with the mound of gravel that had saved his life, slowing the cars momentum before it collided with that crane leg, if it hadn't been there, he wouldn't have been either. He opened his blurred eyes to two figures dressed as dock workers, it took a moment or two for his vision to clear as consciousness returned with a rush of the cold night air and the pattering of cold rain on his coat. The two men were smoking as they talked, passing a bottle of whiskey between them to ward off the chill air from the Hudson.

He tried to speak but his words came out in a slow slur as he realised he was handcuffed to an old chair at the end of a jetty, with his own handcuffs.

One of the men in dungarees wore a leather work cap and he turned to Rainey as he passed the bottle back to his friend. "Welcome back, Detective Rainey! Sharpe's going to be pleased you're out of the picture! You're too nosey for your own good, my friend," he said blowing smoke into the big man's bleeding face.

"What about Toledo?" asked the other man.

"Don't worry about it! The House just named Sharpe as the King of Spades, I'm sure that pleases him after the feds turned him down!" He laughed still looking into Rainey's groggy face. "Bet you didn't see that coming Detective, that you were working for a man who was working for us!"

"Toledo's not going to like this!" the other man said fearfully.

"Who cares? We have our orders, Sharpe outranks Toledo now, unless you want to tell him you would rather follow that small man?" he said standing up to face his friend.

Rainey had sat listening to them and fitting the pieces together as his head cleared even more. He subtly tried to squirm free of his cuffs, trying to remember what Marvo had told him all those years ago. He was very aware of the cold, dark water lapping against the jetty's legs and his heart started to fill with fear as the man with the cap flicked his cigarette into the river and moved toward him smiling. "Time to say goodnight, Detective!" he said grinning.

"STOP!" yelled a well-mannered voice behind them. "What are you doing? I told you, I don't want him dead, he's far more useful alive!"

"Sorry, Toledo but orders are orders," the man with the cap replied, as the small man approached nursing his neck.

"I am in charge here and unless you don't want me to…" Toledo was interrupted by the man with the cap as he shoved Rainey's shoulders hard tipping him and the chair backwards into the shockingly cold water with a huge splash.

The shock was intense as he hit the water and he sank with a mass of bubbles as they spiralled up to the surface, from his nostrils and around the chair. As he sank into the cold black depths, holding his breath whilst trying to overcome the chilling blow from the water. He tried hard not to vent any more air as he watched the lights from the quayside swallowed by the gurgling rush of watery darkness. He struggled with his bonds as the watery silence filled his ears and the depths enveloped him in a chill embrace. As he sank he saw three flashes on the surface, two in rapid succession and then a third as another body hit the water with a thundering shower of bubbles. It streamed its way down to him, the black figure's arms by its sides as it exhaled in a wake of watery fizz. As the back legs of the chair struck the bottom of the river in a near soundless bump of silt, the figure of a man reached him, he circled around his back as Rainey struggled to hold his breath. The man was fiddling with his handcuffs and a moment later he was free. The dark silhouette tugged at him to swim towards the surface. He swam up after kicking his legs from the bottom in a gurgling mass of shifting water, shedding his big coat, as they both rose toward the surface. They both erupted from the rain soaked motion of the river with a gasp of air, coughing and spluttering with steaming breath. The figure sank back under weakly, but Rainey grabbed the man and pulled him back to the surface. As with a pain racked body, Rainey hauled him up to a lower platform that led down from the jetty, and then with a great effort heaved himself up with a rush of water from his body. They both lay next to each other, gasping and coughing in the cold air as their breath streamed away into the night. They lay there exhausted as the rain hissed around them on the lower wooden platform.

It was a while before he could roll over to observe his rescuer, the man had been shot in the back through his chest and blood ran freely from the wound, Rainey put his big hand on it to maintain pressure but he knew without hospital assistance the wound would turn fatal. His vision was clearing from the pain and shock of the water and he stared disbelievingly at the body next to him.

It was Toledo.

He looked different though, his usual pasty skin had somehow melted away in the water and although one of his eyes was still black, the other was blue, his beard was also missing, and Rainey couldn't believe it, as Toledo smiled at him.

"Penny?" he said with his mouth open.

"Hey, handsome!" she breathed weakly. "I'll bet you're surprised to see me, right?"

"I don't understand!" he stammered as he lay there astounded.

"You're a good friend, Rainey, but a lousy detective." She smiled. "I tried to keep you out of this, I like you and I didn't want you getting hurt. My sister was the one you call the Phantom, she's the reason I'm here and…" She stopped as she coughed again, this time there was blood. He pulled her close as he sat up holding her to keep her warm.

"Don't tire yourself honey, it's going to be OK. They'll be here soon and we will get you to hospital," he told her. Although his mind was still trying to cope with what he knew, his words had come out weakly and he hadn't believed them himself.

"You're a terrible liar, Jasper! If only I had the time to explain. I'm so tired, so cold!" she said putting her head against his chest. He thought for a moment and his head was spinning.

"You don't need to honey, give me your hand and just relax OK?"

"Gypsy magic?" she joked weakly.

"Yeah something like that," he answered as he took her hand in his and concentrated.

A whisper of sand later and he was there, they were young and caught up with the fantasies of every growing girl, they were going to be famous with pink feathered wraps and sequined dresses, outshining all the stars in Hollywood. They swapped costumes and make-up, everything from changing woman to man to fake injuries and bruises. The bedroom was their theatre and the world was waiting. The vision shifted then to their father as they both watched through a crack in the door, arguing with a sharply dressed man that slavery was wrong whether it be from a House of Cards to The White House in Washington. The sharply dressed man in his black coat with purple silk inside had told him that there just wasn't enough money to do what he wanted. But the House could help, with the giving of one of his daughters for training; she would be given a decent life and God willing returned when slavery was abolished. Conrad looked at him furiously as the vision changed again. It was Penny's sister giving her vow to the House of Cards in front of a hooded man on a black throne, the symbol of a king on his dark velvet cloak.

"I am Mary Hartley and I renounce all here before you, my king. All I have I will give to the House to serve this cause and may there be a reckoning for my father's end!" she spoke as Penny looked on in the back row of the shadows, watching the veiled purple lady, observing her.

The vision shifted again as Rainey saw Penny try to talk sense into her at the run down Majestic theatre the night that he himself had shot her. The vision changed for the last time as Penny stood in the mirror dressed as Toledo, consoling herself and steeling herself of what she had to do next. "Do it for your sister!" she had said to herself, as the rush of sand pulled him gently back to the rain filled jetty.

"That's how you knew!" she said, her voice just a harsh whisper. "We just wanted to stop them, both of them. They tore our world apart; it was their turn to suffer! There's a boat called Star Shine just down the dock from here, it was our father's boat, the keys are in my pocket; in the galley you'll find a suitcase filled with the money I took from the House as payment for my services. I want you to use it, Rainey, bring the Black King and the Purple Lady to their knees, when they finish this game they will only move on to another city and play there. Sharpe knew that you were a threat and wanted you dead by her orders. Smack him one for me, OK?" she said coughing.

"It's as good as done, Penny," he said smiling.

"My name is Eva Hartley. I took the name of the prostitute that the House disposed of, for not making her move, it was never solved."

Rainey remembered the file he had read.

She looked at him, her face was pale and reached into her pocket, pulling out the cuckoo broach. "Sorry, I took it. I saw it when I was at your place trying to throw you a curveball, when I thought you had found me out. It's why I lied to you about the bank job. Was it your wife's?" she asked.

"No, it was my mother's," he said softly, as sirens echoed in the distance.

"She's got great taste! Do me a favour, Rainey; don't drink anymore of that paint stripper!" she said.

He smiled down at her as the rain smeared the rest of her make-up and the life left her eyes as she stared up at him.

"I won't, Eva Hartley. I Promise," he told her. He crouched over her lifeless body crying like a broken-hearted child, as the cuckoo broach slipped from his hand onto the wooden decking.

It wasn't long after that a host of police cars stormed the docks, their blaze of multi-red lights flashing through and around the night sky. Rainey had walked up to where they were, hovering around his wrecked car, he was soaked and cold to the bone, as Sharpe walked up with Newman holding his umbrella.

"You've done it this time, Rainey! Car chases in the street, endangering people and even dragging poor Peters into this! I want your resignation now!" he barked at him, as a team of policemen looked on.

Rainey turned to him with a shivering smile and smashed him square in the face, Sharpe flew from under his umbrella to land unconscious on the gravel floor.

"Sorry Chief, I didn't bother to sign it!" he said.

Just then Sam's car pulled up with a man handcuffed in the back seat. "Are you, OK?" he asked.

Rainey nodded. "It's about time we left the force, Sam. I've found out that other agendas are going on in the city and Sharpe was a big part of it." He then turned to his fellow officers. "This man is also known as the King of Spades and subverted this department, so that this House of Cards could quietly control the city. I know a lot of you don't understand but it happens to be true."

Sam looked at the men he had worked with for years. "It's true, the man I apprehended told me so under questioning. Take Sharpe away, there's going to be a shakedown in this department, so those involved can start to worry now! Let's go people!" Sam barked.

The officers collected Sharpe and put him in a squad car as Newman dumbly followed with him, they all went about their business taking in what Sam had said.

"When you said questioning, did you mean interrogation?" Rainey asked mildly, as one of the officers placed a blanket around his shoulders.

"Let's just say it took some looking into," Sam replied with a smile. "What will you do now?"

"I think I will open a detective agency. There's still a lot to do before I can bring the House down and I'm not sure I can trust the department to help me! You're welcome to come with me, Sam!" he said.

"Someone's got to watch your back here! Might as well be me!"

"Sam, you have quite the flair for the dramatic!" he said with a smile. "It's nice that I finally have a friend."

"Oh, I see that means as being a friend gives you permission to drive my car!" Sam said as they walked back to it.

"I wasn't thinking anything of the sort, Sam!" Rainey replied in feigned shock.

"You are a terrible liar, Rainey. Do you know that?" Sam laughed.

Rainey stopped and turned back to where the paramedics were carrying Eva's body with a cover on her face, back to an ambulance.

"Yes I know, a friend told me so," he said softly as he walked back to Sam's car, the rain falling from a dark black sky hissing on the black gravel around him.

The End